My Father's

EVALD FLISAR

MY FATHER'S
DREAMS

Translated from the Slovene by
the author and Alan McConnell-Duff

istrosbooks

First published in 2015 by
Istros Books
London, United Kingdom www.istrosbooks.com

Originally published in Slovene as *Velika žival samote*

© Evald Flisar, 2015

The right of Evald Flisar to be identified as the author of this work has been
asserted in accordance with the Copyright, Designs and Patents Act, 1988

Translation © Evald Flisar and Alan McConnell-Duff

Graphic design: Davor Pukljak, Frontispis.hr

ISBN: 978-1-908236-22-7

Printed in England by
CMP (UK), Poole, Dorset www.cmp-up.com

This publication is made possible with the financial assistance of the
Trubar Foundation, Ljubljana, Slovenia

LOTTERY FUNDED · Supported using public funding by **ARTS COUNCIL ENGLAND**

Men don't choose evil because they like it,
but because they mistake it for happiness.
Mary Wollstonecraft

1

It isn't easy to talk of one's early life, even after so many years. However, allowing for lapses of memory, I intend to hold nothing back, otherwise telling the story would be a fruitless exercise. Much of it remains unclear, including why my father shortly after his fiftieth birthday went off his head. That was all the more surprising because he had never given any impression that he was anything other than the sanest person on earth. So, at least, he appeared to those who knew him. And he was known to a great many people: as a country doctor he covered twenty villages and was paid regular visits by patients ranging from pregnant girls to old men requiring colostomies. It is true that the doctor in the neighbouring district was of a friendlier disposition, but my father could boast a much higher rate of cure. That's why he felt that a guarded measure of disdain for one's patients was hardly a crime. Surprisingly, he was exceptionally pleasant to hypochondriacs, for whom he harboured a special feeling of closeness.

In my mother's opinion he could have been a little less pleasant to young pregnant girls, who appeared to be his favourite patients. As far as I remember, that never caused any problems, except once, when a particularly attractive Gypsy girl from a hamlet in the nearby woods came for an examination insufficiently clean. This upset Father so that he locked her into a bathing cabin, releasing her only after she had showered twice and once more for good measure. Although he later denied accusations that he had spent half an hour drying her with a miniscule towel, the Gypsies threatened him with court action until he mollified them with a wad of cash, about half of his monthly salary.

My father was a quiet man, but occasionally he was struck by a fit of anger of such magnitude that he was more shocked by it than anyone else. Usually it was my mother who pushed him over the border of self-restraint, especially when she dared to criticize his 'experiments' in the basement of the health centre. In her opinion he should have refrained from any work that was not part of his duties at the surgery, and devoted the rest of his time, like most husbands, to his family.

"Family?" was his usual response. "One bastard and one feeble-minded woman are hardly a family."

Mother could bear his rudeness only by turning it into a joke. "Everybody's got what they deserve," she would observe with a bitter smile whenever she felt disinclined to argue. Her capacity, not to mention the will, to argue with Father had eventually waned, and they settled for aiming their words past each other, with Father exploding only when he was hit accidentally. But never, not even in the throes of his worst distemper, did he hit Mother, however much I felt that that was what she was trying to get him to do.

Whenever I summon my father to memory I see a tall, slightly stooping gentleman of middle age, with slow, careful movements, somewhat plumper round his waist than he would have wished, yet far from being fat, with a neatly trimmed reddish beard and gently greying hair parted on the side, which made him look younger than he was, always wearing a slightly anxious expression, which could, however, together with the softness of his eyes, unexpectedly leap into a warm, puzzling smile, sufficiently charming for him to be known, especially among the female patients, as the 'handsome doctor'.

It was probably his popularity that irked Mother most, for she desperately wanted his smile to be reserved for herself and me, although I was its happy recipient often enough, most likely because I never argued with Father. Another habit of his that Mother couldn't stand was his natural tendency to be eternally lost in thoughts. Indeed, very often he seemed to be most absent when he was at home, pontificating on God knows what problems or, with eyes closed, completely absorbed in classical music, hardly Mother's favourite.

At first Mother worked as a receptionist at the health centre, but shortly after they married Father talked her into retraining for the position of an accounts clerk with a nearby brick factory. Otherwise, ran his argument, the health centre would begin too resemble 'a family practice'. There was hardly any danger of that, for next to Father and his assistant, Nurse Mary, the health centre also housed a dentist and his assistant, not to mention their common receptionist. It was much more likely that Father began to be bothered by Mother's increasing curiosity about his "experiments" in the basement of the health centre, where he was spending so much of his time. Once he even admitted as much. He said he had nothing to hide, but simply wanted to pursue his research in peace.

"You mustn't think," he would occasionally turn to Mother with a sarcastic smile, "that marrying a doctor automatically confers on you a degree in philosophy. What could a man of science and a housemaid possibly talk about? Wishes are one thing, but fortunately in this world it is abilities through which we realise our potential."

Mother tried her best not to show how lonely she felt. Any objections she found the courage to raise were promptly brushed aside by Father's acid wit, in the face of which she felt transfixed like a small rodent confronted by a deadly snake. Gradually she came to realise that it was much safer to communicate with Father in monosyllables, and to entrust her grievances to me. There were days when she could not stop. With a cigarette perched on her lower lip, dishevelled, with one hand swinging this way and that, and the other firmly on a bottle of Valium in the pocket of her apron, she would cross and re-cross the living room and pile lamentation upon lamentation: that "this man" would send her to an early grave, that she had no one who would "at least try to understand her", that one day she would simply walk out of the house and "drown in the nearby stream", and that, obviously, I must hate her as well, otherwise I would not always "take Father's side", or would, at the very least, grant her an occasional "loving smile".

Evidently I was failing her as much as Father. I, too, was wrapped up in my own world, which was far removed from her notions of an idyllic family life of a country doctor. Whenever I wasn't lost in one of the books I took from Father's library I would wander through the surrounding woods or sit in my room, daydreaming about nothing in particular and everything at the same time. Sometimes I even locked the door, pretending to study for school, while in fact I would be staring out the window, trying to imagine Father at work, examining patients, lancing boils, signing death certificates. And, above all, working on his experiments in the basement, to which he alone had the right of entry.

I loved Father very much. Without him, my growing years would have been lonely and without any mystery. I had no friends at school. Father was the axis around which revolved my joys and expectations. He seemed like a god to me, infallible. I was particularly excited by the smells that hovered about him every time he returned from the surgery: of unusual potions and disinfectants, of unknown acids and bitter-sweet ointments, even – I sometimes felt – of blood and lymphatic fluid, and the aromas of hundreds of illnesses, of which he was able, when we had guests, to talk so convincingly that most of those present instantly developed appropriate symptoms. Father laughed, comfortably at home in the midst of pain and suffering, never succumbing to as much as a cold, as if protected by the spell of a benevolent witch.

One day he invited me for a walk to the edge of the wood above our house, where he spent almost an hour of his precious time talking to me. It was spring and the meadows were overflowing with flowers. Sitting on the trunk of a fallen birch tree, we surveyed the village below us: the grey rectangular building which housed the health centre, the shop, the inn, the houses, mostly farms, the school which perched like a speck of bad conscience among the trees on the opposite slope, and our home below us, half hidden in the luxuriance of the surrounding orchard.

"Look," Father waved his hand. "Life is beautiful. But it is beauty that causes the deepest anxiety."

Then, using mostly learned expressions, yet visually enough, he took the trouble to explain to me step by step the mechanisms of reproduction of the human race and everything surrounding this incredible mystery. He devoted particular care to the ins-and-outs of what he chose to call coitus.

"Sooner or later," he concluded, "the devil will start to tempt you toward the abyss. Don't resist, only be careful not to fall all the way. It's probably not very pleasant at the bottom."

I said nothing. I was thirteen years old. And in any case he had not told me anything new; I had already gleaned all the relevant information, laced with photos and diagrams, from some of the books in his library. But to tell him that would have deprived him of the joy of feeling a responsible father.

Also, I didn't want him to know how many books from his many book shelves I had devoured. Some were probably less than suitable for my age. But ever since I had learned to read, rummaging through Father's extensive library was without a doubt the greatest joy of my life. The school had quickly become a bore and failed to provide the sort of excitement I craved. Everything was the same year after year, teachers were neither witty nor clever, and hours spent in the classroom seemed to be gliding past like in a dream. Not surprisingly – to the great sorrow of Mother – I was not the star pupil. I just couldn't be bothered.

I was average, quiet, invisible.

2

But all that changed on the fateful day when we were asked to write a free composition entitled "What I dreamt last night". The theme was right up my street: I had been having unusual dreams for some time, and I also remembered many of them, certainly enough to choose from. And so I chose the one I felt the teacher would find at least interesting, if not worthy of singling out for exceptional praise. I decided to record the dream as I remembered it, honestly, without frills. Allowing for a few holes in my memory (the events took place twenty years ago), my dream essay read roughly like this:

"I dreamt that my Mother was returning home from the city by train. My father and I discussed whether the way someone died was predetermined by fate, or whether it was a matter of chance. Our reasoning went like this: if the train bringing Mother home gets derailed, she will survive, but only if fate had decreed that she should not die in a train accident; otherwise she will die. But if she does die, this might also be due to chance, simply because she had found herself in the wrong place at the wrong time. So there was no way of telling. Except, suggested Father, if someone deliberately derailed the train. Then, if she remained alive, we could conclude that the time and manner of death are indeed determined by fate. If, on the other hand, she did not survive, death must be a matter of chance for the simple reason that fate would not allow her to die in a train accident if it had decided to dispose of her in a different way. But if fate *wanted* to kill Mother in a train accident, fate itself would cause the train to derail.

"The proposition seemed logical enough, so Father and I hurried along the track all the way to the point at which it passed a deep ravine. There, with a pickaxe, we removed a section of the rail, took shelter behind nearby trees and waited. It didn't take long before the train's whistle sounded just round the corner. Then it all happened much quicker than either of us had expected. One more whistle was heard, sounding almost like a cry for help. Then we heard a horrible squealing and crunching noise as the locomotive jumped the rail and tumbled into the precipice, with the carriages following and with deafening knocks and bangs piling on top of one another at the bottom of the ravine. Less than a minute later only steam could be heard escaping from the pierced boiler of the squashed locomotive. A quick survey of the scene revealed a mountainous pile of twisted metal, resembling a huge, disordered scrap-metal yard, decorated with disembowelled, dismembered or beheaded corpses, amputated limbs, shattered skulls, splattered brains, a few toddlers and even two dogs and three cats.

"Father and I hurried home to await the results of our experiment in front of TV. When the report finally came, it was worse than expected: one hundred and twenty three dead, among them Mother, no survivors. That's how Father and I obtained proof that Mother wasn't destined to die in a different way. But neither was she destined to die in this way, for the train was derailed deliberately by Father and me. So we succeeded in proving that fate doesn't exist, and that everything, including death, is a matter of chance."

I was very proud of my essay. But the teacher, who read it silently in front of the waiting class, grew increasingly red in the face, until, right at the end, he turned deathly pale. He quietly locked the hand-written sheet in his desk without saying a word. But already that same afternoon he turned up at our house and pressed the essay into Mother's reluctant hand.

"Ask your husband to examine his head. I hope, for your sake, that he will find nothing worse than that your son is trying to make a fool of me."

Mother was so shattered by the event, and especially by the contents of my literary endeavour, that she had to take three days off work.

"God help us," she said when she finished reading my essay to Father, who had asked her to do so on account of his alleged inability to decipher my scrawls. "And I had such hopes! This child will amount to nothing!"

"On the contrary," Father immediately put a different view, as was his habit. "A dreamer often turns into a genius."

Winking at me, he added: "Right, Adam?"

I was encouraged by Father's protection. Yet more and more I began to fall prey to an alarming feeling that I was somehow hovering above my life, rather than living it. Almost invariably I was nudged into daydreaming by something I had read. The intensity of the events that would unfold in my turbulent imagination caused a restlessness which would drive me on aimless wanderings across the village meadows and through the nearby woods. In solitude and silence I tried to sweep away the images which multiplied in my head like a tumourous tissue, to make room for new ones, which were already hurling themselves against the membrane of my consciousness. But I could not sweep the old ones away fast enough. So they were pushed by the new ones across the border of wakefulness into dreams. Very soon my nights, too, were swarming with grotesque pictures and curious happenings.

Inevitably it was Mother who first noticed that something wasn't quite right with me. She demanded of Father to give me a thorough examination. But Father was full of ready-made, neatly phrased excuses. He said that for a boy of my age it was normal to live as if dreams were a reality. Wallowing in illusions was no less my right than a chronic feeling of dissatisfaction with he world, which in any case was one of the basic human rights, and so on. Mother took a gamble and accused him straight to his face of a complete lack of interest in the fate of his son, and of selfishness which was a disgrace for a doctor who had any self-respect.

This appeared to have worked. The next day Father decided to subject me to a little professional scrutiny, as he put it. First he wanted to know which books I had borrowed from his library, and from the school library, and from the village library. I mentioned Zane Grey, Dostoevsky, Flaubert, De Sade, Kafka, Goethe, Cervantes, Nabokov and a few others. He seemed astounded by the mixture. He suggested that, for a while at least, I should read books which are read by other boys of my age. But before I could tell him that other boys of my age read hardly any books at all, he had already changed his mind He suggested that I should stop reading altogether, at least for six months. Then he came up with the final solution: I should go on reading whatever I wanted, but should record all my dreams and fantasies in a diary, which he would examine once a week to make sure that I wasn't developing any kind of mental disorder.

Without knowing why, I liked the idea of recording my dreams, and of making them part of my personal history. I bought a yellow notebook and set about the new task without delay. By a strange coincidence, the first dream I recorded was more unusual than any I could remember having.

"In the beginning I found myself returning from school along the path I normally followed. It was early evening and the sky was unusually dark. I walked lost in thoughts, without paying much attention to my surroundings. So I barely noticed the silvery light that gradually spread over the meadows. I became aware of it only when a strange sound appeared in the air above me. It was metallic, yet soft and rustling at the same time. Next I became aware of the presence of an invisible being. At first I tried to ignore the feeling, but suddenly it swept over me with such force that I had to turn. There was nothing. I felt a lump in my throat and my hands went damp with cold sweat.

I began to walk faster. But the nagging feeling that I wasn't alone would not leave me. Suddenly I felt a sharp, stabbing pain a little above my left ankle. Glancing at my feet, I noticed a grey hen whose long, sharp beak had just struck at my ankle for the second time. Then the hen flapped its wings and began to peck at me as if obsessed. I ran off across the meadows without any direction, just to get away from my unexpected attacker. But the hen wouldn't let go of me; it spread ts wings and flapped after me, clawing at my feet, calves, knees, at every exposed part of my legs. I could feel I was bleeding from many wounds. The hen's eyes were unusually bright, and every so often they began to burn with a piercing glow. Its wings were causing a pulsating, rustling murmur which followed me past the edge of the wood and into the valley.

Soon the grey hen was joined by two more, one black, the other white. Now I could also determine the origin of the rustling noise: flying toward me from all directions were multitudes of hens, cackling, screeching, gurgling and producing a variety of other sounds, all of them orchestrated into a metallic murmur that seemed to be sweeping toward me like an approaching flood. From one direction were coming only grey hens, from another white ones, from the third black ones. And not a single rooster among them! Far in the horizon I could see groups of hens rise into the air and sail toward me like dark thunderclouds. The smell of so much poultry soon overpowered me and I sank to the ground, fainting; the last thing I heard was the rush of wings directly above me.

On regaining consciousness I found myself surrounded by endless numbers of quietly crouching hens with their heads drawn back and sunk in their necks. The three different colours had mixed, so the hens now resembled a thick carpet spreading in all directions as far as the eye could see. I rose onto my knees and looked around. Woven into the feathery carpet were myriads of gleaming, freshly laid eggs. I heard a strange crackling sound; little chicks were already pecking their way out of the nearest shells.

Then, right behind me, I heard a noise which was closer to breaking and shattering than gentle crackling. As I turned I saw emerging from a huge egg, larger even than me, a grim-looking, uncommonly robust chick determined to leave its prison as soon as possible. Within moments it swelled right in front of my eyes into a giant hen which lowered its gaping beak toward me, picked me up and swallowed me. Pulsating muscular walls embraced me, pushing me deeper and deeper, until I slid into a moist cavern full of gurgling noises and a thick soup of acids, which burrowed into my body and began to turn it into something horribly different. I could feel my limbs shrinking, my neck extending, my belly swelling, my nose elongating, and then there was a thump, as if the cavern in which all this was happening had fallen and landed on very hard ground.

By this time I was really frightened. I began to press and knock and push against the walls of the cavern to escape its suffocating closeness. There was a crunching noise, something hard suddenly gave way under pressure and my eyes were flooded with silvery light. I was able to take a deep breath – only to find that the over-powering smell of so many hens no longer made me faint, but instead filled me with great excitement. I discovered that I was standing on a pile of pieces of a large eggshell. Without a single thought, instinctively, I bent down, picked them up one by one with my large beak and ate them with a noisy crunching sound. I was so horrified by this act that I opened my mouth to call for help, but the sound I emitted resembled anything but my usual voice. What came from my throat was the crowing of a rooster!

From as far away as I could see my call was answered by a shrill greeting of myriads of hens which were flapping their wings and awaiting my guidance. I shook my feathers, which appeared smooth and shiny, caused my crest to achieve full erection, flapped my awesome wings, took to the air and flew across the meadows. There was a stir among the hens, travelling in concentric waves all the way to the horizon. Beating my wings, I flew majestically in a straight line, followed by perfectly formed black, white and grey battalions of my devoted army of female admirers. This is the beginning of a new era, I thought. My era. I rose even higher, while the hordes of hens behind me converged into dark flying clouds. Raining down from these clouds like balls of hail were millions of eggs, which would cover the planet and enlarge my dominions to the ends of the galaxy. Just rising above the horizon in the east was the sun. My crest swelled even higher: the sun had the shape of an egg."

Of course it had to be Mother who first read the account of my dream. Although I had pushed the dream diary deep under the mattress, she obviously knew where to look. When I came home from school I found her on the sofa with my yellow notebook in her lap, and with tears in her eyes.

"Adam," she looked at me as if someone had just died. "What's happening to you?"

"Nothing, Mother," I shrugged and turned to go to my room.

"Wait! We have to talk before your father gets home."

I paused and waited, staring at the floor. I ignored her request to sit down.

"Adam," she began, making a long pause before finding the words to go on. "Adam, boys of your age are prone to doing something which is not good for their health. But they find it hard to resist. How successful are you in resisting it, Adam?"

I tried to fake a yawn. "I've no idea what you're talking about."

"You have, Adam," she said, "and a very good one, too, so don't pretend. I'm talking about what boys of your age do with their right hand, and about spots they leave everywhere, especially on the sheets that have to be washed by their mothers."

"Peter does it with his left hand," I blurted out, "he is left-handed."

I could almost hear the sound of air being drawn into Mother's lungs. I saw her putting my notebook on the sideboard and rising to her feet. Afraid that she might hit me, I turned to run out of the house – and bumped into Father who had just returned from work.

"Father," I pointed an accusing finger at Mother, "she's read my dream diary."

"Here," she quickly reclaimed the initiative by passing him the notebook, "read for yourself the distortions of your son's mind, and don't reproach me for it, because you brought him up. Whatever I said, you always called feeble-minded."

She pushed him aside so she could pass into the hall, where she clumsily stepped into her tennis shoes and walked out of the house, slamming the door. As Father and I looked out the window we saw her crossing the courtyard to her bicycle, which was leaning against the door of the garage. She mounted it and furiously pedalled off down the gravel driveway to the road.

"You have no right to read his diary!" Father shouted after her, although she was already too far away to hear him. "Are you a doctor? How many times do I have to tell you that you're not!

Apart from that, the boy's at an age when privacy is essential to him!"

Before nightfall Mother quietly returned, as always when she stormed off in anger. Father had used her absence to read, and then carefully read once more, the account of my "rooster dream", frowning here and there, but also emitting a few spontaneous chuckles. After dinner, which Mother prepared in silence, and which we ate in silence, Father cleared his throat and passed his opinion.

He said that this particular dream of mine, like all the others, was a consequence of my premature reading of books which my virgin intellect was unable even to comprehend, let alone absorb their contents in any meaningful way. So the contents had nowhere to go except sink into my subconscious mind, from where they erupted into my dreams in the form of surreal images. At the same time, he continued, my dreams were a classical symptom of sexual awakening. The metaphoric content of my last dream left no doubt about that: I wanted to peck my way out of the shell, which was my childhood, because it had become too small for me. I wanted to grow a crest with which I could command the allegiance of hens, in other words of the female sex, which the rooster, or man, must fecundate according to a biological programme in his genes. The number of eggs in my dream showed very clearly that my urge had reached a critical stage, and that I could lessen the built-up tension only by more frequent and vigorous masturbation.

What followed was the worst quarrel I had ever witnessed between Father and Mother. Insults were flying about like shrapnel on a battlefield. Soon they completely forgot about me, so I slipped out, ran to my room and locked myself in. But even there I couldn't escape the sound of their bellowing voices. I could muffle them slightly, but not completely, by pulling the duvet over my head. Eventually the quarrel ended, like so many before, with Father unleashing the full fury of Wagner on Mother's ears.

I prayed to God to let me stay in my next dream forever.

3

But soon I was having too many dreams, and they began to suffocate me. Daily hallucinations merged with nightmares so imperceptibly that I was finding it harder and harder to draw the line between them. Afraid that I would sink in the burgeoning swamp of my own imagination, I began to flee in the direction of hard reality, grasping at anything that could be seen, felt, heard, or smelled. Soon I became so oversensitive that I registered the slightest rustle, the tiniest change in light, the least noticeable smell.

Suspecting that I had caught one of the strange diseases Father treated at his surgery, I sought his help. I described the symptoms. He took my temperature and blood pressure. Then he listened with a stethoscope to my heart, breathing, and abdominal gurgles. Finally, with a broad smile, he slapped me on the back and said that I had obviously become a victim of the "hypertrophy of the senses". This was not connected with any serious illness, such as a brain tumour, which might cause similar symptoms; it was simply another aspect of my growing up, and would start leaving me in due time.

But before it started to leave, it intensified. I became particularly aware of it one day in the middle of summer as I lay in the grass near the village stream. I was intoxicated by the sweetish smell of hay which was drying on the meadows. The meadows spread along the stream all the way to the hills, where fields of wheat surrounded them.

Although I lay in the grass, covering my face with both hands, I could not escape the sights and sounds of my surroundings. It was like watching a movie on the screen of my retina: not only the overflowing hay carts and rhythmic movements of the loaders, but also the glum, sweaty horses, twitching their backs because of swarming flies, the women who tried to wipe perspiration off their foreheads with the backs of their equally sweaty hands, and the men who drank warm cider from clay pots and then, in turn, strode to the nearest bushes for a leisurely pee.

I could hear the gentle rustling of alder-trees lining the stream, and a timid breeze caressed every so often my neck and the soles of my feet. A horse neighed in the distance, one of the hay carts creaked and wobbled over the uneven ground, one of the loaders was swearing and cracking his whip. Simultaneously I heard the children who were splashing about in the stream, their shrieks, and laughter, and cries. The water was not deep enough for proper swimming, but one could do many other things, such as jumping into it out of the overhanging trees, or teasing the girls if you were a boy, or the other way round.

Suddenly I became aware of someone lying nearby in the grass. It was Eve. She was looking away from me and towards the stream; or so, at least, I thought, for I was afraid of turning my head and meeting her eyes. When the clock in the church on top of the hill began to strike twelve, the bathing children started to climb out of the stream and run toward the village to their homes. It was the same every day. By the twelfth strike most were already far away, their shouts barely audible. Hot oppressive silence began to creep over the meadows; the loaders, too, had decided to take a rest. Then a body moved in the grass a short distance away. I was dumbstruck: Eve had not left!

This time I could not resist looking in her direction. She was lying in the grass on her stomach, nibbling at a fresh stalk of sorrel. Every so often she bent her legs at the knees and swung them backwards and forwards in the air. Her teeth were white, even and dense, and she had a red bikini, composed of a tiny bra and even tinier pants.

For a long time we lay there without a word. The breeze had died down and the sun began to burn with a vengeance. The stream was barely audible; the sound of the flowing water reminded me of a stuck fly persistently beating its wings. My head was getting heavier by the minute, my limbs were stiffening, and eyelids were closing against my will. Suddenly I heard her voice, bright and sonorous.

"Aren't you hot?"

Of course I was, and could have said so, but my throat felt as if suddenly filled with jelly. All I could produce was a hesitant "aaahhhr", hardly the sort of eloquence with which to impress a girl. Convinced that she did not understand what I meant, I gathered all my energy to explain that *of course* I was hot, very hot, who wouldn't be, and wasn't she as well? But she spoke before I opened my mouth.

"There is shade on the dam. Shall we go there?"

For a while there was silence. During this period, which seemed longer than it probably was, the church clock struck half past twelve. In the meadows behind us, the loaders had resumed work, someone was yelling at a horse. The carts were moving again. The grass around us smelled of dry soil.

"Where?" was the first stupid word I managed to utter.

I knew perfectly well where the old dam was. It was no more than twenty yards away, and hardly a dam at all, just a wall with a flat top, keeping water from the side branch on which there had once been a watermill. The branch was now dry and overgrown by thick bushes, but near the dam there were wide, three-foot walls, overhung by trees. Many a time had I rested in their pleasant shade.

"I'm going," she said.

As she deftly rose to her feet I noticed that the grass had left shallow furrows in the skin of her thighs. (The sight of those gentle marks on her smooth, unblemished skin is what after all these years I remember most, more even than her eyes, lips, or face. I can close my eyes and see those marks as clearly as if they were before me.) As she set off with her girlish swagger toward the dam, I engaged in a brief struggle with myself as to whether to stay or follow, which I promptly lost in favour of the latter. She parted the branches before us and held them so they wouldn't rebound in my face. She was a head taller, although she couldn't have been much older. I was fourteen, and she – fifteen?

"Isn't it nice here?" she asked when we reached our destination. The stiffness in my throat was slowly turning into a full-blown anxiety. I knew how cool the shade on the wall was. The top of the concrete mass, too, was delightfully cold as I stretched out on my stomach. She stretched out next to me; the wall was just wide enough for two. Our breathing seemed a little fast for the amount of energy put into our effort to negotiate the short distance.

"Now we're hidden," she said. "No one can see us, right?"

Suddenly, almost interrupting herself, she exclaimed, "What's that?" And she pressed her forefinger hard at my ribs, right at the centre of my large birthmark.

"Just a wart," I said, jerking away; she was pressing so hard that it hurt.

"Are you ticklish?"

"No!" I said firmly.

"Let me try," she became curious, and she started to tickle the soles of my feet which swayed in the air next to her. My reaction, not unpredictable, delighted her.

"You see!" she shrieked with delight. "And what about here?"

Before I could get away she began to tickle my ribs, the most ticklish part of my body. The involuntary laughter that erupted from my throat sounded much too wild for the way I felt generally. I twisted and tried to push away the exploring fingers of her soft hands, but to no avail. As the muscles of my belly began to hurt from excessive laughter I tried to get hold of her fingers to immobilise them. But she snatched them away every time with great skill, tickling me with a delight which soon began to resemble a desire to torture.

In the end I had to resort to begging. "No more, please, no more!"

She stopped. My head was spinning. I was no longer sure where I was. But the initial distrust had been broken, I ceased to feel her presence as a threat, we sat up and looked at each other relaxed, like very close friends. I could almost feel the joy surging up from my depths, and all the feelings of stiffness had dissipated.

We lay down again, next to each other. Although I'm not a great talker even now, and was even less so at the age of fourteen, I suddenly blossomed into a real babbler. But she had much more to say even so. She talked at length about the adventures of her Grandpa Dominic, a sea captain who had retired to the village of his birth, and with whom she was spending her holidays so that he wouldn't be alone all the time. She boasted that in the city, where she lived with her parents, more things happened in a day than in my village in a year. The village, she said, was a terrible bore.

I talked about the school, and how I felt out of place there, as if condemned to spend years among a tribe of savages, and especially about Father, my hero, who was engaged in conducting far-reaching scientific experiments in the basement. In a year or two, I said, he would allow me to join him, and eventually I, too, would become a doctor.

"Good," she said, "then you'll be allowed to examine me, like your father."

I could not hide my surprise. "My Father examined you?"

She nodded.

"Where?" I asked in a broken voice.

"Here," she said, putting her hand between her legs. She parted them slightly, so that she could cover the triangle of her bikini pants with the palm of her hand.

"Why?" I insisted hoarsely.

"Because it hurt," she said, somewhat surprised. "You never hurt?"

"Not there."

"Well, I do. Women are different," she announced, as if being one already.

"And what did my Father ..." I failed to complete the question.

"My goodness," she expressed surprise at the fact that I seemed to know so little about these things. "He rubbed ointment into it. White ointment. He pushed it deep inside and spread it all around."

"Inside?" my voice broke again.

"Yes, with two fingers," she extended her middle finger and forefinger. "He did a very good job. Took him more than ten minutes. Now it doesn't hurt any more."

Just as I was about to ask if Nurse Mary was present during the treatment, two little girls came running along the upper wall of the dam. They paused, pointing at something in the water and arguing, then carried on and disappeared.

"They were naked," breathed Eve and fell silent.

I wasn't shocked by the fact that the two little girls had nothing on. I was shocked by Eve's use of the word. She seemed to have invested it with a disturbing weight. After some time she asked, and her voice, too, had become slightly hoarse:

"Would you dare to bathe naked?"

It must have been the word dare that helped my vanity to surface above the turbulence of my feelings.

"Of course," I said, as if throwing the words away. "Wouldn't you?"

"If no one saw me."

"Why only then?" my courage grew.

"I don't know," she shrugged. "I'd be embarrassed, I suppose."

"But you aren't in front of my Father."

"He's a doctor."

I felt that a reversal of roles had taken place and that my fear had moved into her, which made me almost burst with self-assurance.

"I wouldn't be embarrassed," I said. "Why should I be?"

"Because someone might see what you have."

"Everybody's got that. Including my father. And your grandpa."

I could feel a slight tremor in my voice, but I did manage, half in despair, to put the decisive question. "Would you be embarrassed if someone saw what you have?"

Promptly, as if she had waited for it, she replied, "I wouldn't mind showing it to someone who showed it to me."

She fell silent and I could feel her body tensing up. The ball was now in my court. The anxiety, mixed with uncontrollable expectation, was almost too much to bear. My throat muscles worked as if I was about to start yodelling. But when I finally uttered the words they sounded quite normal.

"If you wouldn't tell anybody," I set a condition.

"Don't be a dummy," she said. "Of course I wouldn't. And neither should you."

A brief silence followed, with each of us waiting for the other to speak.

"Who'll be first?" she breathed, and looked my straight in the eyes.

Quickly, I averted mine, swallowed an excessive amount of saliva and stared at the upper end of the wall.

"Tell you what," she came up with an idea. "One of us lies on the back without moving, eyes closed. The other pulls off his pants and looks at the thing. Then he puts his hand on it and holds it there for, say, a minute. The other can keep his eyes closed. Shall we?"

I nodded and she agreed to be first.

She removed her bra and stretched out on her back. It was not difficult to pull off her bikini pants; she lifted and twisted her pelvis to help me. She kept her eyes closed. But mine were open wider than ever. Seeing her naked, the first naked girl I had seen lying before me, was like being hit on the head by a soft, yet powerful hammer. Her body was slim, smooth and tanned. I remembered a sentence from one of the books habitually read by Mother: "Her nipples resembled two rosebuds." Eve's nipples resembled more than anything two large birthmarks, very much like the one on my ribs.

I placed my hand on the "thing" between her legs. The brownish lips surrounded by a downy growth of short curly hairs felt unlike anything I had ever touched. They seemed firm and yielding at the same time. I imagined my Father's fingers rubbing ointment deep inside her, and a lump appeared in my throat. I kept my hand there for what seemed like a minute, but was probably longer. She didn't mind. Her cheeks were deeply flushed, her breathing unusually fast. Every now and then she would push the "thing" against my hand in a gentle rubbing motion.

"Tell you what," I whispered. "I will lie on my back with eyes closed. You undress me and touch me in the same way."

I stretched out on my back, closed my eyes and waited. I lifted my pelvis to help her remove my bathing shorts. I kept my eyes tightly shut, but when for a long time nothing happened I decided to look what was wrong. I was struck by a terrible fear that she didn't like what she saw. Just then I felt her fingers gently wrapping themselves round my "thing". This was the first time that fingers other than mine were embracing the part of me to which, in Mother's opinion,

I was devoting too much attention. The fingers felt soft and cool, maybe because my "thing" was so hot and hard. The fingers began to move up and down in the way mine always did.

Suddenly I heard her whispering into my ear, "I know a game we could play."

"What game?" I pretended not to know what she meant.

"The game adults think is reserved for them," she said.

"That's not allowed," I heard myself saying the stupidest thing that came to my mind.

"Man should be free or dead, says my grandpa. He should know, he's been a sailor for thirty years. He's seen things you wouldn't think possible."

"All right," I said.

I had been dreaming of such a moment for so long that I could not understand my sudden hesitation and fear.

She stretched out on her back next to me and asked me to lie on top of her. When I did so, she parted her legs, and I found myself lying between them.

"Now put your thing into mine," she whispered into my ear.

I tried, but it was more difficult than I thought, and I was unsure to what extent I had succeeded. "Is that all right?"

"Of course not, you dummy," she berated me. "Stop poking around the entrance. Push it right in, push harder."

I moved away to get a thrusting distance. Quietly I took a deep breath and then with a sudden motion jerked forward, only to feel horrible pain as I hit something unyielding and my "thing" bent in the middle. Eve, too, uttered a small cry of pain.

As I prepared for another try, I raised my eyes and suddenly saw, standing on the upper end of the wall, my Father, hands in pockets, watching us. I froze. Father came closer and, towering above us, looked at me with a strange glow in his eyes. Now Eve, too, became aware of his presence.

"Oh no," she whispered.

Father pulled his right hand out of the pocket, bent forward and struck me on the face so hard that I fainted.

4

I am not sure to this day for how long I remained unconscious. It could have been minutes, or it could have been half an hour. But during those moments I experienced once again what I had hoped would become a rarity: a highly unusual, vivid dream. In this dream I saw my father lying on the upper end of the dam completely naked, as naked as I had ever seen him. With him was Eve, who was also naked, but that did not surprise me, since I had seen her undressed only a moment earlier. What I found most unusual were their respective positions. Father was lying on his back with both legs outstretched. Eve was crouching above him as though she had just mounted an animal for a ride. She wasn't just crouching: supporting herself with both hands against Father's chest, and with Father's hands tightly clasping her hips, she rhythmically bounced up and down, with an occasional grinding movement in between.

In my dream I had no idea why she was doing that. Her gasping and occasional moaning pointed to a degree of pain, and the expression on her face was tortuously twisted. Yet in spite of that she seemed to me more beautiful than ever, especially when she raised her face, fringed with sweat-soaked blond curls, and under tightly shut eyelids stared into the depths of herself. Usually she opened her eyes only when she lowered her head to look at Father's face, but on one occasion she opened them with the head still raised and looked straight ahead. The eyes seemed dead, glassy, as if staring into emptiness.

Then, suddenly, they sharpened and, startled, looked straight at me. Eve shuddered and her body stopped moving up and down. She seemed confused. But only for a few seconds, then her spasmodic movements resumed with an even greater vigour. Far from averting her gaze, she now deliberately aimed her look directly at me, as if deriving pleasure from this. At one stage she even winked at me, as if letting me know that we were partners in a conspiracy.

Then I sank into darkness again, into a black abyss, which saved me from what I was witnessing.

Out of the darkness I slowly emerged back into the world of consciousness. Rather strangely I found myself exactly where I remembered losing it: on the wall of the dam. I turned my head, expecting to see Father and Eve still there. But I was alone; the only thing moving were the shadows of the tree branches swaying above me in the summer breeze. This happened a long time ago, but I still remember the unfamiliar feeling which swept over me: the feeling of, almost, regret at no longer being able to watch Father and Eve making love (for, awake, I knew only too well what they had done in my dream). This feeling was immediately followed by deep embarrassment at having such a desire. Although the image of them was very much alive in my memory, it was surrounded by misty uncertainty, and I began to wonder whether the whole after-noon had not been a dream, from the moment I thought I became aware of Eve lying next to me in the grass. Maybe she never came to sunbathe near the stream; maybe everything was no more than one of my strange imaginings.

But how did I find myself on the wall of the dam? And why was I naked, with my bathing shorts lying next to me? This did not seem to support my hope. As I slowly walked home, my confusion grew to the point of despair. How could I look Father in the face ever again? I knew he would soon be home; it was Saturday, when he only worked till two. As I was nearing the house I decided that it might be best to run away into the woods and stay there until both Father and Mother began to worry if I was still alive; then, surely, neither of them would dare mentioning anything that might drive me away again. But it was too late: just as I decided to slip past the hedge and run across the fields towards the safety of the nearest beech-trees, I heard the wheels of Father's car on the gravel driveway in front of the house.

"Adam, wait," he shouted.

I ran as fast as I could, but his hands grabbed me from behind just as I reached the edge of the wood. Gasping for breath, we collapsed on the grassy fringe, already in the shade of the nearest trees.

"Adam," Father wheezed and panted above me, "Adam, I'm sorry."

After calming down a bit more, he added, "I'm sorry I hit you."

With his apology, my hope that the whole thing had been a dream was blown away. Suddenly I was filled with dread that all the rest might have been true as well. It was with immense relief that I heard Father say, "What did you dream?"

"People don't dream when they're unconscious," I put my final doubt to the test, "they only dream when they're asleep."

But Father insisted that I had not been fully unconscious, I had merely slipped into some kind of intermediate state, resembling the phase of sleep during which dreams are most vivid. He employed a medical term in support of his theory, REM, rapid eye movement. While we dream, our eyeballs roll around under the eyelids, and that was what he had seen as he bent over me to revive me. Seeing that I was dreaming, he decided not to wake me. It is essential, for the sake of mental well-being, that dreams are not interrupted, especially not if they are in any way unpleasant or shocking. Unpleasant dreams especially are an excellent means of clearing out the garbage which accumulates in the psyche, he concluded.

"So," he returned to what seemed to bother him, "what did you dream?"

I stared at my feet and said nothing. How could I possibly describe the dream I had on the wall of the dam without dying of embarrassment?

"Listen, Adam," he said. "You know I have never hit you before. But this time I had a good reason. Do you realise that?"

Again I said nothing, I merely shrugged.

"I have nothing against your desire to follow your natural drives. This is perfectly normal at your age, and I approve of your efforts to lose virginity. The problem is Eve. She may be a year older than you, but she is still underage. What would her grandfather say, to whom her parents entrusted her in good faith that she would be safe with him? And that's not all. She is my patient. As her doctor

I am responsible for her. Can you imagine what would happen if people learned that the doctor's underage son was having sex with his father's underage patient? You would be sent to a correction school. I would end up in jail."

Silence was all I could offer in reply to that.

"Are you telling me you don't care?"

I shook my head and mumbled something.

"Speak up, so I can hear you," Father said.

I looked up and said clearly and loudly that I did care. But I still didn't dare look him in the eyes. Now even less than before, for now I wouldn't be embarrassed only because I dreamed what I could never tell him, but because he caught me doing things which I would have preferred to do without his seeing it.

"Eve is of course very charming and quite mature for her years," Father said. "But not the sort of girl you should hang out with. She's got a serious problem. I should know, I'm treating her. Even more important: you shouldn't talk about this to Mother. We don't want her to suffer a stroke, do we? There're things men have to keep to themselves. Do we understand each other?"

I said nothing, I merely shrugged. I felt that my dream could much more easily be confided to my dream diary than either to Father or Mother. Suddenly I felt a great need to write it down, and so lessen its burden. I decided not to show my diary to anybody. And I knew where I was going to hide it so that no one would find it.

After some hesitation, Father put his arm round my shoulders and gently drew me toward him. "Still writing your diary?"

I looked at my feet again and shook my head. I said I had thrown the yellow notebook into the well in the school's courtyard on the last day of school. I no longer dreamed as often as I used to, so I had nothing to write about. In any case my dreams had become very vague and fragmented, I hardly remembered any of them. There seemed to be no point in recording senseless jumble, I said.

"Actually," Father said, "it wasn't a bad idea to get rid of that diary. If you dream anything unusual, anything that bothers you, you can always tell me, and we'll talk about it. Not as doctor and patient, but as father and son."

I nodded.

"Shall we go home then?" Father said and got to his feet, visibly relieved.

I could never clearly remember the days that followed. From the very start they were suffused with a strange, surreal mist in which, with the passing of time, things and events became less and less discernible, let alone definable. Very often I felt that I wasn't seeing things with my eyes, but rather feeling them with some inner tentacles. Although I recorded every detail in my dream diary, it was difficult to tell from these notes whether I was talking about dreams, hallucinations or real events. Only I knew, or thought I knew, that I was describing dreams, and only I knew that dreams were about Father and Eve. In fact, after the event on the wall of the dam I hardly dreamed about anything else. If I did, it was always at night, and forgotten so fast that any diary entry would not exceed a couple of lines.

Dreams about Father and Eve usually took possession of me in the afternoon or early evening, always without any indication that they were about to start, as if I had been sucked into sleep by an invisible power which pushed me over the edge of a precipice into an abyss; it was like suddenly fainting. Occasionally I dreamed standing up, but my presence in the dream was always that of an observer. So I could not really say that I dreamed about Father and Eve. I dreamed about us, myself included, with the only difference that they weren't aware of my presence, whereas I registered every movement, gesture, step, look or sigh of theirs, every expression on their faces.

That was largely due to the fact that my "hypertrophy of the senses" had somehow extended its power from the waking state into my dreams. I could smell the dusty straw in the barns in which I stealthily watched them – as though the straw were real and I were really there. I could hear the straw's crackling and rustling as Father and Eve, engaged in a strange wrestling match, intertwined

33

like mortal enemies, rolled about, emitting spine-tingling moans. I could feel the evening dew on the grass, and hear the racket of crickets in the harvested fields, and the subdued barking of dogs at the houses they passed on their way to a hiding place.

In my dreams they were getting together wherever and whenever they could, in the nearby wood, in the meadows lining the stream, even, late in the evening, in the orchard behind our house, where they ran the risk of being discovered by Mother. Although in the dreams I sometimes wished that this would happen, it never did; they were only dreams, after all, and I had no control over the way they unfolded.

Regardless of where they met, their coupling ritual always followed certain rules. First Eve would look around to find the most suitable spot, then she would pull off her panties and throw them away, then she would lie down on her back and pull her skirt up to her navel. My Father would kneel down before her and spend a few moments watching her. She would bend her legs at the knees and sway with either one or the other this way or that. Then, still on his knees, Father would move closer, wrapping her legs round his waist. Then they would start. I could never tell how long they remained together. Sometimes it seemed like a very long time, and often, spying on them from behind the bushes, I would get bored. But I could not simply get up and leave; in a dream I had no will of my own.

In one of the dreams they met at their usual place in the wood, took off their clothes and pranced about naked among the trees. Father had to catch her, tie her hands with his trouser belt, then tie her with his necktie to the nearest tree; only then was he allowed to push against her from behind and start with his thrusting movements. To see each other naked, and to be able to play hide-and-seek among the trees like two little children, seemed to provide them with greater pleasure and more excitement than the actual coupling. But not me. I still felt the greatest thrill when Father slid into her and she uttered a shuddering sigh or even a subdued cry; then my heart took off as if trying to beat its way out of my chest. This lasted until Eve's features drew into a distorted expression of pain and she dug her nails into Father's back.

But all this was only the stuff of my curiously repetitive dreams, which I faithfully recorded in my secret diary. The dreams were so frequent and my descriptions so elaborate that I soon filled the notebook and had to buy a new one, a red one this time, which I gave the title *Dreams II*. I never asked myself why I was making all those detailed notes, considering that I could never ever show them to anyone, certainly not to Father and least of all Mother. Nor did I read them myself, except every now and then to add a detail or two, for some things, strangely, I could only remember later.

Quite often I found that recording the dreams gave me more pleasure than the actual dream itself. Why it was so, and why the dreams had become such an obsession, and why occasionally I caught myself wishing they would become even more frequent, I could not tell. From time to time I fell pray to the haunting thought that Mother's fears were coming true and that I was indeed slipping dangerously toward the edge of madness. As for Eve, after the event on the dam I did not dare approach her any more; I wouldn't know what to say to her.

5

There was only one person I could confide my dreams to, and that person lived in the basement of the health centre where Father conducted his secret experiments. Because the door was not only locked, but padlocked as well, Father had no idea that I, too, had access to the kingdom he had created under the wooden floors of the surgery. There was an old stove in the cellar for which, before the installation of central heating, coal was needed, and coal used to reach the basement down a chute which, from the outside, had long ago been hidden from view by a confusion of brambles, while in the basement it was partly obscured by a pile of old furniture. Getting into the basement required no greater skill than squeezing through the brambles and sliding down the chute. Getting out required some ingenuity: putting a half-broken chair in front of the chute, climbing onto it, than climbing up the dusty chute using elbows and knees, taking care not to get scratched or too filthy in the process.

The basement was filled with so much rubbish that one could hardly move around. There was everything, from broken crutches and rusty surgical instruments to old, moth-eaten medical manuals, dusty files of patients long dead, and seemingly endless amounts of medicines which had passed their "use by" date. But the basement also contained other, less everyday objects. Screwed to the wall and reaching all the way to the ceiling were wooden shelves which contained, standing next to one another, round, rectangular and triangular glass jars with corks or aluminium lids, some no bigger than ten inches, others extending over two feet. In those jars, preserved in formaldehyde, were the trophies of God knows who's surgical undertakings: an amputated child's hand, a few appendices, a cut-off ear, a foot with crushed toes, a kidney, a pancreas and two excised tumours. Sitting at the bottom of one of the larger jars, resembling a small overturned canon on wheels, was a male sexual organ, amputated with both testicles.

My Father was not a surgeon, merely a general practitioner, but often, whether for his own pleasure or as a matter of urgency, he undertook work which, by all the rules of medical practice, he should have left to others. Even so, most of the preserved organs could not have been removed by him, for the health centre lacked the necessary equipment. He could only have cut them out of dead or dying people, something he would hardly have found a good reason to do. After all, floating in one of the jars was a human heart. But I never doubted that it was he who had handled most of the aborted embryos and dead-born foetuses which lined the longest shelf. There were at least twelve in the glass jars, and every so often they would be joined by a new one. Some were so small they resembled large tadpoles rather than early shapes of anything human; others already had eyes and beginnings of limbs, noses, ears, tiny fingers. Some were almost fully developed, prematurely born little people of recognizable sex, with eyes which, even behind closed lids, seemed to express something akin to astonishment.

Although they were all fascinating, there was one that I really liked. In fact, I liked him more than anything else in the world, including Father, whom I liked a lot. This particular foetus was more developed than any of the others, and had a larger than usual head. Although I knew that this was not possible, he seemed to be smiling and his frog-like eyes appeared to be half open. In a strange way he seemed almost alive. He was also the only one with a name; stuck to the jar in which he floated was a label on which someone had scrawled, "Abortus, the son of Mary and Joseph."

Joseph, or Joe as he was known, was my Father. Mary was my Mother. There could be no doubt that Abortus was my dead-born little brother. It often seemed to me that there was a certain resemblance between us, especially around the mouth and the eyes. We seemed to be looking at the world in a similar way: shyly, with concealed wonder, yet stubbornly at the same time. Father and Mother never mentioned the possibility of my not remaining an only child. Nor did I know if Abortus inhabited Mother's womb before or after me. This was something we never talked about. What was clear, however, was the fact that I could have had a brother. After a while I came to believe that I did have one, simply one that could not leave his little home. And because he could not, it was my brotherly duty to live part of my life for him.

The main reason I kept coming to the basement was to talk to Abortus and tell him what was happening in the world outside. The things we did. Because part of my life was his I always felt that whatever happened, happened to both of us. I would tell him how the physics teacher made fun of us in front of the whole class. How during a football match Luke deliberately aimed a kick at our shins. How we combed our hair with a comb we found lying on Katya's table, and how she lifted the comb in the air so the whole of the class could see it, and shouted: "Does anyone have a strong disinfectant?" As long as I believed that half of my life belonged to Abortus I felt only half the anxiety I would have felt otherwise. Of course I also shared pleasant things with him. Whenever Minny smiled at me in the school corridor, or the headmaster said that if I had less imagination and a trifle more perseverance I would definitely be the star pupil, I did not keep this to myself. I shared it with my little brother as though it was meant for him anyway, and I was no more than a transmitting agent.

We communicated in a seemingly simple way: I would talk, and he would listen. He would respond in his own way. At first I would connect the barely noticeable changes in his expression with the light which was coming in through the window, and which shifted every time a cloud passed before the sun or the tree branches swayed in the wind. But gradually I began to see the almost imperceptible movement of shadow and light round his mouth and eyes as his way of responding to my words. Step by step, we developed a way of communicating which enabled us to exchange information and views on a number of things. In my loneliness there was no one I could talk to as openly as I could to my little brother. Talking to Father was interesting, but not always warm or intimate; it seemed to me that for anything like that Father simply couldn't find the time. Which, of course, did not mean he didn't love me. Talking to Mother was mostly a pain: because of her incessant worrying about the respectability of our family she would mostly instruct me what to do and what not to do, while I would defy her by remaining stubbornly silent. Only to Abortus could I talk as an equal, as one half to the other half; only together were we a complete person.

So it seemed natural to entrust to him for safekeeping my dream diary, not only *Dreams I* but also *Dreams II*. In the tight space between the jar and the wall behind it the two notebooks were completely hidden from view by Abortus and the liquid surrounding him. The chances of Father stumbling upon them accidentally were practically non-existent. In any case he wasn't coming to the basement because of Abortus or other glass jars. The objects of his scientific research were housed in containers which lined the shelves on the other side of the window. These containers, also made of glass, had unusual shapes: one was formed into a spiral, another was pinched in the middle like a sand-glass, the third resembled a large smoking pipe, and yet another a canon on two large wheels. There were others, less definable, resembling cucumbers, mushrooms, pears, elephants. Every so often a new surprisingly shaped container would appear on the shelf; Father was getting them by special order from the nearby glass-works.

All these containers housed tiny trees, mushrooms and other, more unusual botanical specimens, all of them grown to fit the shape of their particular glass enclosure. The spiral container housed a little pine tree which had spiralled into the most unusual growth I had ever seen, shocking in its deformation and yet profoundly beautiful. The sand-glass contained a cactus pinched in the middle, and the smoking pipe was the home of the most unusual tropical flower, with a pink blossom sticking out of the sucking end, and a blue one out of the filling end. There were some rather witty jokes among Father's achievements in the art of growing bonsai: a mushroom grown to resemble a cucumber, and a cucumber grown to resemble a mushroom.

I knew that this was "the art of growing bonsai" because lying on one of the shelves nearby was a large book bearing such a title. I had leafed through it many times. But no photograph in the book showed anything remotely as beautiful as the strange living things produced by Father during his secret sojourns in the basement.

It is only now, after all these years, that I am beginning to understand why he refused to share those experiments with Mother and me, or with anyone else for that matter. He probably felt just as alone in the world as I did, and needed something that would be his, and only his, in the same way that I wouldn't tell anybody about my little brother. Any knowledge about our special relationship by a third party would have robbed it of its uniqueness, which lay in the fact that Abortus, such as I saw him, was the product of my imagination, my artwork. In the same way Father must have felt that letting others in on his solitary efforts to add beauty of his own design to an ugly world would have spoiled the beauty and made his efforts commonplace.

I did not feel any guilt for being a party to his secret. I was too young to know what I know now. What I did feel was that Father's obsession was for him the only way to counterbalance the ugliness of disease and death he had to face daily in his surgery.

Like the basement, Father's surgery, too, was not ̣
a boy of my ingenuity. The health centre was situateᴗ
building in which cracks and gaps were appearing all oʋ
place. One such gap I had discovered by accident a year oɪ
earlier when I climbed the fire-escape stairs at the side of the building and squeezed through a wooden hatch into the loft. Between
the wall of the chimney and the wooden ceiling I found a gap wide
enough to offer me a good view of the surgery below. Since then
I had spent many an hour observing Father at work, sometimes
even missing school, for I preferred to get acquainted with biology
and anatomy in a more direct way.

The gap was a little too small to offer me the view of the entire
room, but the examining table was right below, next to the wall of
the chimney. A little further on, close to the door, I could see part
of another table, which belonged to Nurse Mary. It was covered
by an incredible jumble of medical files and pills and ointments
in various types of packaging, all mixed together in an appalling
way. Sometimes Nurse Mary had to sift through the disarray for
ten minutes before she managed to locate the file for the patient
already stretched out on the examining table, while Father accompanied her frantic search with his usual cynical remarks, tired of
having to repeat them day after day.

As a doctor my Father was never at a loss for words. In fact he
talked incessantly, while Nurse Mary, being the quiet type, contrib-
uted little more than an occasional "yes, doctor" or "no, doctor",
which, when they were alone in the room, became "yes" or "no".
To his patients, regardless of their age, sex or rank, Father talked in
the tone of someone who was aware of his position of power, and
determined to exploit it to the full. Humorously berating those who
disregarded his advice seemed to be one of the greatest pleasures
of his life. But he could also be patient and kind, and would spend

tes explaining to a hard-of-hearing old lady how often and in
t manner to take the pills he prescribed. Sometimes he would
that three times in a row. It was at moments like those that I real-
sed how good my father really was, and how his oddities were no
more than harmless traits of someone who, because of his extraordinary abilities, could not possibly behave like an ordinary mortal.

Peering through the gap in the ceiling, I managed to witness
so many unusual things that eventually there was nothing much
left that could shock me. I would see examinations during which
Father would peer inside female sexual organs through a long
tube; I would see broken limbs, hips, and jaws; I would see der-
matitis and gangrene and the birth of children, where my Father
was always eager to assist, although Nurse Mary was also a quali-
fied midwife. I would see children with mumps, chicken-pox and
boils on their behinds; I would see people fainting after a single
injection, followed by revival attempts that sometimes lasted an
hour. I would see wounds from which blood was gushing in spurts.
I would see nails in skulls and slit throats, and mad people who
at the top of their voice shouted words no one could understand.
And children, battered almost to death by their parents.

Inevitably there came the moment when things began to repeat
themselves, and when the odour of blood and decay started to turn
me off. Sometimes, peering through the gap in the ceiling, I would
doze off, especially during summer, when the air in the loft grew
unbearably hot. Or I would suddenly start feeling dizzy, believing
that I was actually dreaming what I thought I saw in the surgery.
When I began to have frequent and very visual dreams about Father
and Eve, and the line between the inner and outer worlds started
to fade, this went a step further and very often it seemed to me that
even my presence in the loft was no more than a dream.

I knew it was only a matter of time before Father and Eve
appeared in my dream in the surgery. Little did I know that this
would happen only three days after I entrusted my dream diary to
Abortus. Nurse Mary walked out into the waiting room to usher in
the next patient, but returned to tell Father, "Eve is here."

Father winced and shot an angry look at the door. "I told her to come at two," he said, glancing at his wrist watch. "Ask her to wait another ten minutes."

As Nurse Mary obligingly turned to carry out Father's instructions, Eve walked into the surgery. In fact, I remember it to this day; she floated rather than walked into the room, deeply tanned from the sun, wearing leather sandals, a very short skirt and a T-shirt which barely covered her navel. Her blond curls looked unwashed and uncombed.

"We agreed you'd come at two," Father tried to sound stern, pretending to be the kind of doctor he wasn't.

"It is almost two," Eve replied. "I can't wait any more."

Nurse Mary moved to her desk and gave herself something to do with prescriptions and files. Father rose and took a few steps round the surgery.

"You're not registered here," he said. "I'm doing a favour to your grandpa. You're supposed to come when I've finished with my regular patients."

He stopped in front of Eve. Although I wasn't quite sure, it seemed to me that he made a meaningful nod in the direction of Nurse Mary.

"I can't wait any more," Eve said in a soft, half enticing, half pleading voice.

After some hesitation Father said, "Nurse, please tell Burger to wait a little. Go to the dispensary and mix that ointment for him, you know the one I mean, for the warts. The one I promised him last time."

Nurse Mary put down the file she seemed to be studying for no particular reason and in a rather stiff-backed manner replied, "That'll take time, doctor, that ointment has ten ingredients."

"Well, then," Father said, "all the more reason not to waste any more time, wouldn't you say?" And he looked at her, every inch a man of authority.

Nurse Mary, poised for further objections, melted like a piece of lard in the sun. As soon as she closed the door behind her, Father turned to Eve. "Didn't we say – "

"Give it to me," she interrupted him, "or I'll start screaming!"

Father said nothing; he just kept looking at her. Then he walked to the door and turned the key in the lock. Putting his right arm round Eve's waist he lifted her, light as a feather, onto the examining table. A satisfied laughter burbled from her mouth. As she swung her legs backwards and forwards, one of her sandals slipped off and fell on the floor. For some moments Father disappeared from my area of vision. While he wasn't there I kept looking at Eve's brown legs and deeply tanned shoulders.

When Father reappeared he was holding a syringe with a long needle. I expected Eve to wince and draw back, but she willingly extended her arm, letting her head fall back a little, with eyes closed and the lines of her face composed into an expectation of pleasure. With a movement perfected by years of practice, Father pushed the needle into her vein and slowly pressed on the plunger to push all of the clear liquid into Eve's circulation system. Eve uttered a sigh of relief. Father threw the used syringe into the rubbish bin and held his head in his hands.

"This shouldn't be happening," he said, more to himself than to her. "I'm a good man. Why am I doing this?"

Eve slid off the examining table and ended up on her knees. She unbuttoned Father's fly, reached inside and pulled out Father's penis, which she put in her mouth and started to suck. This was the first time I saw anything like it; it had never even occurred to me that things like that could be done. I felt a pleasant wave of hope sweeping over me; the beauty of the world awaiting me had gained another dimension. What I also felt very strongly was that none of this was really happening; it was merely a dream to be recorded in my diary and read out to Abortus, so that he, too, would feel excited about being alive.

Just then Father looked up and twisted his face into an expression of strange discomfort. He seemed to be looking straight at the gap in the ceiling, and through it at me. "Help me," he breathed. "You, who are above me, help me, please."

7

There were moments when I wished I could discuss my dreams with Father. At least he should be able to tell me at what point they began and how long they lasted before dissolving back into ordinary wakefulness. But how could I admit to him that I had lied about throwing my diary in the well? How could I possibly tell him that I was having these dreams almost daily, and always about him and Eve? How would I describe the details? Not only Mother, he, too, would begin to suspect that I was gradually losing my mind. And then, being a doctor, he would feel obliged to treat me. He would drive the vein-throbbing dreams from my head, and I would be left with nothing.

I had become so suffused with my dream world that, without it, I would feel as if I had been robbed of half of my life. I still dreamed about other things as well, but not half as exciting. The unexciting, confusing, nightmarish dreams I normally had at night, mostly before I woke up in the morning. Erotic dreams, by contrast, would come on without warning at any time, mostly in daytime. The manner in which they sucked me in was sometimes abrupt, very much like an ambush, while at other times they would slowly, and almost imperceptibly, merge with my endless daydreaming. Maybe it was all due to the summer heat, in which I never felt fully awake but seemed to float through the days as if wrapped in a swarm of images. Would I be able to, if I suddenly came upon Father and Eve, tell with certainty whether I was seeing them in a dream, imagination or reality? Very soon I began to doubt that.

I knew that sooner or later this would be put to the test. When, late one afternoon, sitting near the edge of the wood above our house, I tried to imagine Father and Eve sneaking through the brambles into the shade under the oak trees, I was not particularly surprised when I felt a pair of soft hands being placed over my eyes from behind; I knew they were Eve's before I even touched them. This was confirmed by her teasing laughter. The only thing that surprised me when she removed her hands was that I couldn't see Father. She was alone. In my dreams they were always together.

"Pinch me," I begged her. "Come on, pinch me, I want to see if it hurts."

First she pinched my left cheek, then the right one; after the first pinch I still wasn't sure, but the second one hurt beyond any doubt.

"You're real," I said, suddenly feeling a wave of fear. A huge lump formed in my throat. I couldn't say another word. Crouching in front me, she was so close that her sun-tanned legs, misty blue eyes, slightly parted pink lips, and especially arms carelessly thrown over her knees filled me with the pain of such uncommon longing that I had to avert my eyes. She was looking at me with the expression of someone who had just caught a strange animal, nothing dangerous, just a little rabbit she managed to trap, and which she could let go immediately or after she had some fun listening to the pounding of its heart.

"Are you afraid?" she asked.

I shook my head. Suddenly regaining the power of speech, I said, "I thought you weren't real."

"Who is, anyway?" she composed her features into an expression of profound importance. These could hardly have been her words. I vaguely remembered Father once saying something similar: who can claim to be real in a world which, as proved by the physicists, is composed mostly of emptiness? Did they talk about such matters in my dreams? Or in the surgery? She was after all, as Father had said, a patient of his. My confusion grew.

"It's so hot," she said. "Why don't we go down to the stream? Have a splash and cool off. Lie in the shade on that wall."

"No," I pounced as if stung by a bee. Not on that wall, I wanted to say, but what I said was, "Not today."

She stood up and sighed as if at a loss what to do.

"Then why don't you come home with me, to meet Grandpa Dominic?"

This sounded more attractive and far less dangerous. But still I couldn't make up my mind. Without another word she moved off. Treading softly with her bare feet, she floated towards the nearest trees. As soon as she reached the shade, she turned and with a curved forefinger beckoned me to follow. She was wearing a short blue skirt which barely covered her thighs, the same one she had in my dream about the events in Father's surgery. But the T-shirt was different, white and suffused with the sweet smell of her sweat, with long sleeves which only just covered her elbows. Her shoulders were broader than her hips. If it wasn't for her softly rounded thighs and gently undulating breasts, her body would have looked more like a boy's than a girl's.

"Come," she grew impatient, "you'll see grandpa's statues from Africa."

She walked on and soon vanished among the trees. I jumped to my feet and followed her along the path which twisted its way under the intertwined branches of alder-trees towards the part of the wood dominated by extremely tall fir and pine trees. There the sun rays shone through the gaps in the congestion of needles, and danced on the mossy ground in the rhythm of the breeze which was inducing the branches above to stir in an exciting, disorderly fashion. The rays danced caressingly around Eve's hurrying feet which led us deeper and deeper into the wood, to the grassy path where I had already been in my dreams, and which led across a flowery meadow to the foot-bridge which took us across a dry stream-bed to the dusty road which led up an incline to Grandpa Dominic's house.

Along the way Eve picked up a stick, part of a rotting branch. As we walked on, she swung it in the air, twisted it in a circling motion above her head, thumped the ground with it, made thrusting motions as if preparing to throw a lance, and used it for checking the path before her while pretending to be blind. Once or twice she scratched her back with it, and three times she placed it on her shoulder as if carrying a heavy club. Twice she leaned on it as she waited for me to catch up. But I always slowed down when I saw her waiting, while she, reassured that I followed, turned to walk on.

As I watched her swagger and hop before me, her image began to merge with the scenes from my dreams, and suddenly I saw Father, too, walking alongside her in front of me, although I knew that he wasn't there. As though they belonged together. As though she on her own, and especially alone with me, represented a burden I felt too weak to carry and wanted to get rid of it before it grew heavier.

It was the middle of August and not even the breeze, streaming gently from the valley below, could soften the oppressive heat. As we emerged from among the trees on to the road which led between the orchards on the right and the wood on the left to Grandpa Dominic's house higher up, I felt the sun on my head like the blow of a heavy fist. I could barely move my legs any more. Eve, on the other hand, remained light as a deer, prancing about in front of me like a hyperactive child, walking now backwards now forwards, then zigzagging from left to right, or whirling about like a peg-top about to lose balance and topple over, almost drunkenly, with her head thrown back so that her hair fluttered around her like a soft-feathered bird. The air was thick with the smells of hay, freshly cut grass, tall virgin grass, hundreds of different flowers, manure, cherries and pine needles, everything joined into the stunning aroma of the lazy summer day.

But as we approached the house, still half-hidden behind the trees, I noticed, behind its gleaming sun-lit facade, an area of darkness. Nestling behind the top of the hill above the house, resembling the shadow of a dangerous beast, was a huge bulk of blackness which was already reaching into the orchard behind the house. I realised that from behind the hill a storm was on its way, one of those summer storms that brew up within minutes and from a single cloud flare up into earth-shaking thunder, hissing downpours and frightening displays of lightning. I was glad we were nearing the house; there was nothing I feared more than thunder and lightning.

Our house had a lightning-conductor, fixed to the roof at Mother's request by one of Father's patients. Mother was just as afraid of storms as I was, if not more. But I could see no such protection on the roof of Grandpa Dominic's house; if struck by lightning, we would burn to death in it. And that was what I suddenly thought would happen; why else would Eve have invited me home at that particular moment? But she was already opening the door, and I would have hated to be taken for a coward.

I followed her into the hall. The sunlight entering through the side window lay on the dusty wooden floor like an exhausted unfamiliar animal. Forcing its way through the window on the opposite side was the blackness of the approaching storm. I could almost feel the cool air that was accompanying it. The rest of Grandpa Dominic's house had also become the battleground of darkness and light. At the uncertain frontline of quivering shadows and sunlight the pieces of furniture gave the impression of being twisted and strangely malformed: the wardrobes weren't straight, but leaned dangerously as if about to topple over, tables bulged in the middle, chairs were flattened or elongated, and everywhere I could sense the crouching figures of invisible beings which accompanied our progress through the rooms with the unbroken attention of guardian spirits.

Hanging on the walls next to spears, daggers and painted wooden shields I saw ancient-looking charts of the world and individual continents, mostly of Africa, framed yellowed photographs of ships and harbours, two portraits of Grandpa Dominic in his uniform of a merchant navy captain, and one of his parents, to whose house he had returned after retiring from the sea some years before these events. Dust and disorder reigned supreme in the rooms whose purpose had long ago ceased to be evident. Everywhere I looked there were books, stacked or piled up wherever there was room, on tables and side tables, under them, on chairs and sofas, on top of an old bread-oven, on wooden benches, even on shelves which contained mostly other objects, unusually shaped old clocks, compasses, copper and clay vessels of every shape and size, broken picture frames, rolled-up charts and posters. Large and small iron chests were covered by plastic bags which contained everything from photographs and letters to gloves, stuffed parrots, rolls of tobacco and cigar boxes. The air smelled of a mixture of damp, dust and unusual spices which couldn't be seen, but they may have been in the kitchen where we didn't go.

As we passed the open door of an untidy bathroom, I saw a flicker of lightning outside the paint-glass window, followed immediately by another. The storm had arrived.

"Where is your grandpa?" I wanted to know.

"Asleep, as usual," Eve replied and took me by the hand. "Are you afraid?" she asked as she led me up a wide staircase to the first floor.

I shook my head, but she sang out, "Poor little Adam is afraid."

The first floor of the spacious old house was even more crammed. While many things had no doubt been brought by Grandpa Dominic from his many voyages, others must have been there for ages, belonging to grandpa's parents or even grandparents. The house was a veritable museum of unsorted oddities. That's why I was all the more surprised when, at the end of the corridor, Eve pulled me into a room which was not only tidy and neat, but also clean, without a speck of dust anywhere, with the air sweet and fresh, not only because of an open window but because of the scents emanating from tiny bottles on top of the sideboard. The bed was covered with a soft, light brown blanket on top of which, squeezed between the pillow and the wall, sat a large teddy bear. It seemed a little out of place in the room of a fifteen-year old girl.

"I don't like sleeping alone," she explained. "I must hold onto something. Otherwise I, too, get afraid."

Suddenly a fiery tongue of lightning reached through the window and licked us all over like a vicious dog. Somewhere behind the hill there was a clap of thunder. The trees in the orchard stirred and began to sway violently in all directions; the wind was bringing the first raindrops, which were landing on the leaves like large tears.

"But never as afraid as you," she added when she saw my face, which must have turned completely white. She closed the window. The rain was fast turning into a downpour and the wind was already blowing it into the room.

52

8

She sat on the bed with her legs crossed, and patted the blanket beside her; that was where she wanted me to sit, right next to her. I hesitated. I approached the bed very carefully, as if ready to bolt at any moment, and sat down on the edge, more leaning against it than sitting on it.

"Tell me about yourself," she commanded. She placed her elbows on her knees and cupped her hands under her chin. She pressed her fingers against her cheeks, which made her pout.

"There is nothing to tell," I said. "Nothing interesting."

"You know what?" she said. "You're boring. But I like you anyway. I like you because I'm bored and need to talk to someone my age. I'll show you something."

She bent over the edge of the bed and reached under it, pulling out a plastic bag of photographs. She poured them out onto the blanket and rummaged among them until they seemed in a bigger mess than before. She made a soft, patronising gesture with her hand.

"My life. Not very long, but already quite rich. Others write diaries, I collect pics."

She watched me intently to see how I would react. But all I managed was a nod and a faint smile. I couldn't relax: I was waiting with horror for the next bolt of lightning, the next rumble of thunder. I wanted to be ready, because this time I wanted to show her that I wasn't afraid. She picked out a few snaps and stacked them up in a little pile. Then, one after another, she began to hand them to me, after examining each with a thoughtful smile. It was obvious that she wasn't showing them for the first time; for each she had a ready-made commentary. On the first one I saw her in a group of schoolmates, with three teachers sitting in front.

"End of school-year," she said. "I'm off to grammar school in the autumn. My dad is a bank manager, he wants me to become very clever and educated and all that. The boy on my left used to be my lover. Very helpful, he would do anything to please me. But he will go to some kind of commercial school, he had very poor marks. So our paths are diverging, as they say."

She said that with unconcealed pride, as if 'diverging' was her personal achievement; one of them, for it soon became obvious that all the photographs she had selected were one way or another connected with facts or events that she hoped would impress me.

"My gang," she passed me the next one.

Leaning against a crumbling wall of an old building in strikingly arrogant poses, right under the graffiti "Fuck off...", I saw three skinheads trying to look aggressive. Eve was crouching in front of them on the pavement, holding a piece of cardboard on which someone had scrawled, "...or get fucked."

I could almost feel her eyes burrowing into me to discover how deeply impressed I was. But I wasn't really. I wanted to say that at my school we also had hooligans, yet I felt no particular desire to appear with them on a photograph. But she couldn't contain herself, she continued before I opened my mouth.

"Nick, Vick, Mick and I, who was called Little Pick. We terrified not only the school, but the whole city quarter. For a while we stole car badges. Must have collected a thousand. Then we poured tar into our teachers' letter-boxes. We were the first at our school to smoke marijuana. Have you ever tried?"

Without waiting for an answer she handed me the next photo. On this she was alone, seemingly on a nudist beach, stretched out on wet, compact sand, leaning on it with her right elbow. Her left leg was slightly raised and bent at the knee. The fingers of her left hand were resting on the downy mound above her "thing". In the lower left corner, a frothy edge of the sea could be seen moving towards her. She was smiling, and the photographer had caught her just as she produced a naughty wink.

"My favourite," she said. "Taken by Mother's cousin. Three years ago he tried to rape me. No one knows, of course, so keep it to yourself."

She pulled the photo from my hand and looked at it with an expression of pride and approval.

"A super snap. I have more than one copy. Once I sent one to my math's teacher who forced me to take a repeat exam. Want to know what I wrote on the back? 'Have a wank, you dirty old man.' I thought he would go straight to the headmaster, but he didn't. And I passed the exam without any trouble."

Before she could hand me the next photo the room was lit up as if by a thousand spotlights. Judging by the sound above, the lightning must have struck very close, if not the house itself. It didn't sound like thunder; it was more like the sky being rent apart from one end to the other. There was a clatter of broken glass, something heavy landed on hard ground and was smashed to pieces, but all this could have been caused by the wind which was turning into a hurricane: the tree tops in the orchard were flailing about like a flock of large birds that took to the air but were unable to fly away.

"Enough of that," she said, piling all the photographs back in the plastic bag. "I can see when someone's not really interested." Leaning over the edge of the bed, she pushed the plastic bag out of view. Then she suddenly leapt off the bed, pulled off her T-shirt and dropped it on the floor.

"It's unbearably hot. Won't you take your clothes off?"

She managed to remove her skirt and panties in a single move. She tossed them in the direction of her teddy bear and looked at me visibly annoyed. No doubt she was used to having whims and desires fulfilled instantly.

"Do you really want to stay a virgin forever?" she asked. "Or is my body not good enough for you?"

Her naked body was certainly stunning, but it was so self-assured that it frightened me. Besides, my attention was suddenly drawn to a bluish mark in the crook of her arm. I was suddenly faced by an equation that I couldn't work out. If my Father gave her injections only in my dreams, why did she have needle marks now, when I wasn't dreaming? Or *was* I dreaming? Or did Father really treat her, and was that injection in my dream a coincidence? Had he not told me that she was his patient, and gave that as the main reason why I shouldn't go near her? I was very confused. As she reached out to touch me I could see very clearly that the mark was composed of traces of many needle pricks.

"You're such a bore," she said. "Don't you know how to have fun?"

The next moment the room was lit up once again, but this time the lightning flickered in the rhythm of stroboscopic lights, with Eve's body pulsating in front of me as though we had suddenly found ourselves in a discotheque. Thunder became a deep rumble which didn't stop but slowly intensified. I bolted out of the room and ran down the corridor. The rumble followed me all the way down the stairs to the ground floor, where it seemed to be coming from the cellar below. As I desperately tried to find a way out I suddenly came upon a sight that made me freeze.

Standing next to the window, outside which the trees swayed in the storm like giant moths, I saw a tall, dignified old man with a wavy grey beard, dressed in a dark-blue sea captain's uniform, erect and with shoulders thrust back, with a silver-lined cap on his head, with golden stripes on the sleeves of his well-fitting jacket, holding a burning cigar in one hand and a telescope in the other. Sensing my presence, he slowly turned. This wasn't the first time I saw Grandpa Dominic, "the old sentimental codger", as he was referred to by Father, but never before had I seen him in uniform, and never had he looked so beautiful, almost like a god who had crossed the sea to rescue a shipwrecked soul.

"You're Adam," he gave me a pleasant smile. "The doctor's son."

I nodded and moved towards him. Although the rumble had ceased I felt that he alone could protect me. For a while his warm eyes rested on me with frank curiosity. His beard was very long; it must have taken him years to grow it. He leaned forward a little as if unable to see me in the semi-darkness. Then he straightened up, put the cigar to his lips and drew on it, and puffed the smoke toward the invisible ceiling.

"Don't be afraid," he said, in a voice which was surprisingly soft for a man of his size. "This little fury is nothing compared to the storms I survived at sea. But one must always be ready." He weighed the telescope in his hand, as though he had been using it to observe conditions far in the horizon, and not merely the flailing branches in the orchard, the nearest of which kept scraping at the window pane.

"Sit down," he waved with the cigar toward the wicker chair in front of the window. "Tell me what's troubling you."

He made four measured steps across the room and sank into an armchair next to a large oak table. He placed the telescope on top of a pile of old newspapers. He clenched the cigar with his teeth and with the thumb and forefinger rolled it from side to side as it glowed in the dark.

Suddenly the room was lit up by lightning. At that moment I saw, lined against the wall behind him, the statues of African gods he had collected on his many sea trips. The statues about which almost everyone in the village had made at least one derisory or stupid remark, although no one had ever seen them. Some villagers even claimed that the old man was a witch and should be forbidden to come to the shop. There were twelve gods, standing next to one another, all two metres tall, with very long noses, with stumps instead of arms, some with huge breasts, others with jutting penises, all with white painted eyes which seemed to follow my every move. Captain Dominic sat in front of them like an interpreter of their thoughts, and of my thoughts for their benefit, an intermediary between their sea of eternity and my little island of restlessness. I felt that these gods knew the tiniest secret, and would not take kindly to anyone pretending in front of them.

"Dreams," I said. "I'm troubled by evil dreams."

There was a moment of silence. Outside, too, it grew very quiet; as if the storm had been forced to take a deep breath, as if thunder were afraid to interrupt Grandpa Dominic's answer. There were two flashes of lightning without any thunder, and in their light I could see that the black gods, too, were waiting in great suspense. It seemed that the whole of creation wanted to hear what the captain would say.

Finally, flicking ashes off the end of the cigar with his middle finger, he said very simply, "I'm listening."

I understood his words as an order. So I began. Nothing could stop me. I told him everything from the beginning, everything I had already told my little brother Abortus and written down in my diary. I described what happened on the wall of the dam, and all the dreams that followed, up to the last one in Father's surgery. I spoke rapidly, with words tumbling over one another, and a couple of times Grandpa Dominic had to remind me, "Slowly, Adam, slowly."

I resumed my story, retelling it by adding more details, as if afraid that otherwise he wouldn't believe it. But every time there was a flash of lightning I saw that he listened with great attention, even forgetting to smoke his cigar. I could see that the gods behind him listened just as intently, and that their eyes slowly narrowed until finally their whiteness faded and they remained standing there as if my story had killed them.

"You really are drowning," said the old captain. "And not a ship in sight."

From the corner of my eye I suddenly noticed that he wasn't alone in listening to my breathless words. Standing in the corridor, half hidden behind the door post, was Eve, whose eyes, during one of the flashes of lightning, glowed like the eyes of a wild cat.

9

For the next three days Father behaved very strangely. Even Mother noticed the shadow of some secret worry that seemed to have descended upon him. He was detached and twice as explosive as usual: a shirt button, refusing to yield immediately to his hasty fingers, was enough to make him livid. He stopped reading and listening to classical records, he stayed at work longer than was his habit, and when he returned he wandered around the orchard with hands in his pockets, pausing occasionally to stare at the ground in front of his feet. Once, through the window in my room, I saw him sitting on the step of the garden shed, nervously smoking a cigarette, the first time I ever saw him doing that. A few times I caught him watching me from the corner of his eye, but mostly he moved about the house as if trying to avoid me.

In the morning I heard him slip in the bathroom while showering; there was a thud, followed by a loud curse. Then I heard Mother hurrying from the bedroom to see what had happened. I heard them talking behind the closed door for almost ten minutes. She was trying to comfort him, while his voice seemed almost meek compared to his usual authoritative tone. Later that day he returned from work with a large plaster above his left eye and with the look of murder in his eyes, softened by almost pitiful bitterness. I felt sorry for him, especially in the evening when he remained sitting in front of the telly without watching it, with arms hanging loosely over the sides of the armchair, staring at the carpet and occasionally at the door, as if waiting for someone to come and tell him what was happening, and why.

Three days later we received a visitor, a gaunt man with a nervous gait and abrupt, awkward gestures. The top of his head was completely bald, but attached to the back of it was a dry growth of greying, mousy hair reaching all the way to his shoulders and leaving on his jacket scattered traces of dandruff. He was failing to make a good impression in several other ways: he walked by swaying his hips as if tip-toeing, and when he listened he thrust his head forward as if afraid that he might not catch every word. Before speaking, however, he jerked it backwards, and the tip of his tongue pushed its way through the gap in his teeth as if making sure it was safe to open his mouth. His first sentence was always followed by short, abrupt laughter, which could mean either that he considered himself to be witty or that he didn't quite mean what he said. He seemed to be permanently on guard; as if afraid that someone might throw a rotten egg in his face.

That might have been happening to him at the grammar school in the nearby town, where he was supposed to teach psychology. Mother, who was obliged to cook dinner for this unpalatable guest, expressed serious misgivings about the possibility of this being true. She said that the man had lost his medical licence for abusing a female patient at a mental institution where he worked as a psychiatrist. Would anyone employ a person like that? No, he was making ends meet with a private psychoanalytic practice. To see what success he is having with that, she said pointedly, we need only to look at the state of his clothes, which are worse than the worst worn by anyone in the village.

"Not to mention the state of the old jalopy in which he arrived," she concluded.

The invitation to dinner had come from Father, who had described the man as a friend from his student days, then a young medical prodigy with a special talent for interpreting dreams. Life had evidently not been very kind to him, quite the contrary, but fortunately it had left this special ability of his completely intact. "After all he writes articles on the subject of dreams for various publications," Father had said.

The man turned up early and Mother and I had to suffer him for an hour. Mother spent most of the time in the kitchen, while he stealthily moved about the living room like a hungry grey spider.

"Unbelievable," he kept winking at me and rubbing his hands together, dislodging dry skin flakes which descended slowly like petals to the floor. "Unbelievable, these dreams of yours. A historical oddity, I dare say."

I felt increasingly stiff. It was evident that any conversation during or after dinner would revolve around me, and I found it unusual that Father hadn't bothered to warn me of something so highly unpleasant. As soon as we finished soup, Dr. Kleindienst, as the man with dandruff was called, abandoned the small talk about weather, summer and good old times, and embarked on what was, no doubt in collusion with Father, the real aim of his visit.

"In all my years of psychoanalytic practice," he said, "I have never come across a case where a patient – and I use the word advisedly – would be bombarded with the same dream night after night. Let alone a patient unable to tell dreams apart from reality."

"But that's been happening to Adam for quite some time," Father said. "Hasn't it?" he turned to Mother, who nodded without any detectable conviction.

"Hasn't it, Adam?" Father turned to me, as if eager for us to present a common front to Dr. Kleindienst, like a closely-knit family.

I, too, nodded. Father and Mother obviously knew that I hadn't stopped dreaming; it would be useless to pretend. What wasn't clear was whether they knew the contents of my dreams. That seemed impossible. My dream diaries were safe with Abortus, he would never betray me. Unless, of course, it was Eve. But wouldn't she be too embarrassed to talk to her doctor about what she heard me tell Grandpa Dominic?

While Mother fetched steaks, chips and salad, Father and Dr. Kleindienst embarked on an exchange of increasingly learned opinions. I don't remember the exact words they used, but the following is my best shot at a reconstruction.

"I've never accepted Freud's notion that dreams are a facade behind which their true meaning lies hidden," stated the visitor, weighing a glass of wine in his hand as if to emphasize the thrust of his words.

"Neither have I", Father said.

"The idea that the meaning of a dream is known to the unconscious, but may only enter the conscious mind camouflaged as a symbol, is manifestly wrong."

"Yes," Father nodded.

"Dreams are a part of nature, and nature has no intention to cheat, it merely expreses something as best it can, in the form of confused images."

Dr. Kleindienst began to chew a piece of veal steak, holding knife and fork in his half raised hands as if trying to defend his point of view. But Father said nothing. Dr. Kleindienst swallowed the chewed piece of veal and washed it down with a whole glass of wine. Then he continued.

"I compare dreams to a screen on which the unconscious projects its inner drama. When we dream, the conflicts and mis-understandings among the forces of the unconscious appear on the screen in the shape of strange images."

"Yes," Father said, "but if my boy dreams that he has changed into a rooster, that doesn't mean that he would like to become one. It means something else altogether. According to Freud it is one thing, according to Jung it is quite another. And if he keeps dreaming about sexually explicit scenes, the kind he may be day-dreaming about when he is awake, this could mean a hundred different things. But none as important as the fact that he dreams about them night after night, and even in daytime, in fact every time he falls asleep."

"Quite," Dr. Kleindienst opened his mouth. I wasn't sure, but it seemed that dandruff could be seen even on the piece of beef he was about to stuff into his mouth.

"Quite," he repeated after swallowing it, "the language the unconscious invents to transmit its contents to the conscious mind can be startling, to say the least. Freud, for example, never explicitly analysed sexual dreams. But he claimed that most dreams were caused by repressed desires, most often sexual."

He looked at me across the table and winked as if trying to tell me not to worry: my secret was safe with him. The he held out his glass and Father dutifully refilled it. They had finished a bottle, and Father went to the kitchen to open a new one.

For a few moments Dr. Kleindienst, Mother and I remained alone at the table. After a tense silence, Mother, while cutting her stake, scraped with her knife against the bottom of the plate, causing Dr. Kleindienst to wince and direct a censorious look at her.

"Can this be cured?" Mother said. "That's all I want to know. Because this must, this simply must stop."

"What's interesting," Dr. Kleindienst assumed a didactic tone, "is that treating everything from a to Z is not always the sensible option. Dreaming profusely doesn't necessarily mean that there is something wrong with the boy. Maybe he is just bored. Maybe it's a sign of incipient genius. It could also be – he is, after all, of that age – an aspect of sexual awakening, which is sometimes accompanied by full-blown hallucinations. On the other hand, it could also be, yes – "

"The beginning of schizophrenia?" Mother looked at him sharply.

"Madam," Dr. Kleindienst glanced toward the kitchen, wondering how much longer Father would take, for obviously he had realised that, on his own, he would be no match for Mother, "to think of the worst possibility first is a sign, and please forgive me for saying so, of that exaggerated motherly concern which often itself causes the problems that are the reason for worrying. I don't mean that Adam's dreams could be a result of anything like that, certainly not, all I'm saying ... this steak is excellent, Madam, quite exceptional ... what I'm saying is that we know less about dreams than we like to imagine. Dreams are the last great mystery of the Universe. We can only guess at what they mean, and I'm afraid it'll never be any different."

"Then what is the point of your being here?" Mother decided to become rude. "We could easily have referred the boy to the nearest Gypsy fortune teller, they also interpret dreams. Why did we not think of that?"

Dr Kleindienst was visibly relieved when he saw Father returning. He almost fell of his chair as he held out his empty glass to have it refilled. He couldn't even wait for my Father to fill it up; as soon as it was half full he pulled his hand back and drained it.

"For me," he stressed, again addressing only Father, "the most important thing is that, according to Jung, the archetypal contents are almost invariably expressed in metaphors. When speaking of dreams we're moving, and I speak from experience, in the world of poetry, a law unto itself, often shocking, yet closely linked to what we could call reality."

"As for me," Mother abruptly pushed her chair away as she got up, "I'm moving in the world of ledgers and balances and common sense, at least I try to. So I hope you'll understand if I tell you that I've started to lose the thread of your learned debate. I'll wash up instead. You carry on."

She cleared the table and carried the dishes to the kitchen, but left the door open so that she wouldn't miss any words. At the same time Father and Dr. Kleindienst raised their voices as if trying to make sure that she wouldn't.

"Brain is a funny thing," said Dr. Kleindienst. "Similar symptoms could be caused by a tumour. I'm afraid, Joseph, that you'll have to examine the boy and exclude that possibility. But no doubt you have done so already."

Mother appeared from the kitchen as if prompted. She didn't come into the dining room; she remained in the doorway, nervously wiping a plate.

"Well?" she demanded of Father. "Have you excluded that possibility?"

Father poured himself a glass of wine, the tenth that evening, and raised it to his lips. Over the glass he gave me a look which conveyed what I took to be a plea for help. He took a sip, put the glass down and said, "Of course I have, I'm a doctor, am I not, that was the first possibility I considered."

Mother took a step toward the table; she stopped wiping the plate and let it hang in her hand, pressing the cloth against her stomach as if trying to quell a cramp. "And what were the other possibilities?"

"Don't expect me to give you clinical details," Father snapped, "you'd hardly know what I was talking about, or have you studied medicine without telling me?"

"No," Mother replied and turned on her heel like a soldier, "I have not. Nor have I ever been struck off the register." And she marched off into the kitchen, holding the plate as if about to throw it at someone's head.

"Madam," Dr. Kleindienst leaned toward the door like a huge praying mantis, "brain can be damaged by quite ordinary events. Falling from a tree, for example. Walking into a lamppost. Being hit by a ball during a game of soccer. By eating poisoned mushrooms. The human brain is the last great mystery in the Universe."

"You said this of dreams a moment ago," Mother returned without the plate and the cloth; now she had a glass of wine in her hand.

"Same thing," Dr. Kleindienst jerked his head sideways as if resenting having to simplify his words for the sake of an ill-educated woman; he looked at Father with an expression that was not far from pity.

"In any case, if I may say so, Madam, considering that your dinner was very good, it is your husband, the doctor, who should be the final arbiter in these matters. It's true that Adam is your son, too, but we're facing things here that are unusual even for the profession."

Mother looked at him as if she had never heard anything so half-baked. Then she asked me if I had ever fallen from a tree, banged my head against anything, had a ball thrown at me or anything else that could have caused damage to my brain. I said I couldn't remember any such events; all I could say was that a certain dream of mine began to repeat itself after Father had hit me and I lost consciousness. But I couldn't say that Father's blow really damaged my brain; as far as I was concerned there seemed nothing wrong with it.

I realised at once that I should not have mentioned the episode on the dam; I could see that by the look in Father's eyes. But it was too late.

"It was nothing, really," I quickly added.

"Of course it was nothing," Father dismissed the whole thing.

"In fact I didn't lose consciousness, it only seemed so, because of the heat," I said.

"You can't damage someone's brain by slapping their face," Father concluded.

"Just a minute," Mother said and put her still untouched glass of wine on the table. "I understand less and less. No surprising, really, being no more than an unschooled accounts clerk."

"Don't exaggerate," Father said.

"And you stop treating me as if I were a fool!" Mother shouted. I could see tears in her eyes. "You come to me and say, listen, Adam hasn't stopped dreaming. He dreams in the middle of the day, and some of his dreams keep coming back. It could be serious. Then you invite a friend who is supposed to know about such things, a dream expert, you call him. Then you both try to convince me that this could be due to brain damage. Now, suddenly, you're trying to convince me of the exact opposite. And finally I even learn that you slapped Adam. When? Why?"

"Hardly worth mentioning," Father waved his hand.

"I want to know," Mother insisted, with tears now streaming down her cheeks.

"Have I no right to slap my fourteen-year old son if I think that'll do him good? Tell me. Am I, or am I not his Father? Because you, on the other hand, keep bugging and criticising him. Adam take off you shoes, Adam put on your shoes, Adam where have you been, Adam where're you going, Adam why don't you eat, Adam what's that you're reading, Adam what are those marks on your sheet, Adam why are you shaming me in front of the teachers? Have you ever thought he might be seeking refuge in dreams to escape your incessant nagging?"

Their faces were only three inches apart. I could see that one of Mother's tears fell on the back of the hand with which Father was gripping the edge of the table. Although he winced slightly, he tried to give the impression that he was not aware of what happened.

Mother straightened up, reached for her glass and drained it. She refilled it from the bottle on the table and picked it up with her right hand, while awkwardly wiping the tears off her face with the back of the left one. Then she walked back into the kitchen, stooped under the weight of emotion. She left the door open. I thought I heard a loud sob, but then everything was quiet again.

Father shrugged, and Dr. Kleindienst shook his head in sympathy. They both looked at me. I reached under the table and pretended to fiddle with the straps of my sandals.

"Can I go to my room?" I asked.

"No," Father said, "we're talking about you."

As they continued, they mentioned a number of things, including the possibility that my dreams could be an outcome of fantasy. Not of passive dreaming, but of *phantasie* in the ancient Greek sense of the word. Dr. Kleindienst pulled a biro from his breast pocket and wrote it down on his paper napkin. He explained that to ancient Greeks the word meant "that which makes visible". The psychological function of fantasy was to make visible the hidden dynamics of the unconscious part of the human psyche. In other words, the sexual scenes I relived in my mind might not be dreams in the true sense of the word. They might be something that my unconscious beamed into my conscious mind to acquaint me with the desires I would not otherwise dare admit. They concluded with an agreement that, while there was no reason to panic, I should be kept under observation, in case treatment became necessary at some later stage.

Finally, late in the evening, Father invited Dr. Kleindienst to go with him to the health centre where he wanted to show him some of his experiments. I followed them out and watched them get into their cars. It was pleasantly cool; the sky was filled with stars, and hanging low above the hills was a sliver of the moon. It was nearly midnight. As two pairs of rear lights flickered off and disappeared among the trees, I suddenly became aware of Mother standing behind me. I turned and saw that she was smoking again. This time her decision to give up cigarettes had lasted no more than a week. Her breath smelled of alcohol. Next to the wine, she must have secretly devoured half a bottle of brandy.

"Tell me about your dreams," she said.

It came out all by itself, without any desire on my part to lie. In fact, I was more astonished by the words I heard myself saying than she must have been. I said that Father had every reason to worry. My dreams, which might indeed be fantasies rather than dreams, were horrible, perverse. They concerned the sea captain's granddaughter, who was spending her holidays with him. We were meeting wherever we could, in the nearby wood, in the orchard behind the house, in the bushes on the banks of the stream. And when we were together, we took off our clothes and did those things.

"What things?" Mother held her breath.

"Those that are done by lovers in films," I said. "Those thrusting movements. That joining of mouths and other parts of the body."

Mother exhaled very loudly and said nothing for almost a minute. Then she said, hoarsely, "Oh my God, Adam. Is that what it is?"

10

During my second visit to Grandpa Dominic's house I said nothing for a long time. And neither did he; sitting in his chair in front of the African gods he patiently waited for me to start, giving me an occasional encouraging smile. He could feel that I wanted to tell him something, and I was grateful to him for not hurrying me. I just couldn't find the right words. A beam of sunlight shone through the window right on his face, the only beam that managed to penetrate the gloom of the cluttered room, and in it's light grandpa's face glowed with the serene expression of a saint.

This time he wasn't wearing his uniform. He was wearing badly creased linen trousers and an unbuttoned striped shirt, which revealed a yellowish sweat-soaked vest. I could easily have mistaken him for someone else. His bearing was different, too; he wasn't as upright as he had been during the storm. His face, exposed to sunlight, appeared much older. I didn't know it then, but remembering these events now I realise that he must have been well into his eighties.

He reached for a cigar, slowly lit it, put out the flame of the match with a quick jerk of the wrist, and pushed the match into the breast pocket of his shirt. The smoke spiralled upward through the beam of light, vanishing in the darkness under the ceiling. Eve wasn't at home; we were alone in the big house. Alone with the African gods, which stood quietly behind Grandpa Dominic's back, barely visible in semi-darkness.

"How are the dreams?" he finally broke the silence. "Still there?"

I nodded. "But not for much longer. Father's decided I need to be cured of them."

"Oh," he said and quickly drew on the cigar, expelling the smoke somewhere to the left, toward the rolled-up sea charts under the table.

"When was that?"

I told him that this happened a few days ago, following the visit of Dr. Kleindienst, the acknowledged dream expert. After talking to him in the basement of the health centre, where they went after dinner at our house, Father realised, perhaps at Dr. Kleindienst's suggestion, that dreams were gradually washing me away from the shores of reality, and that I had to be pulled back before it was too late. This, Father could only do by sneaking into one of my dreams, so we could dream it together. He could then slowly guide me away from it and back to the normal state.

"But is that possible?" demanded Grandpa Dominic, sounding as if the question had slipped from his tongue. "Still, your Father is a doctor," he corrected himself. "He should know, shouldn't he? The question is, do *you* believe that's possible?"

I said I saw no reason not to believe my father. Having practiced medicine for so many years, he must surely have cured cases far worse than mine.

"Of course," muttered Grandpa Dominic.

He kept looking at me in a thoughtful way. He had smoked his cigar to the end, but did not dispose of the butt; instead he kept twisting it fitfully in his fingers.

"The dream is not an isolated psychic event completely cut from daily life," I said. "If it seems so to us, that is only an illusion that arises from our lack of understanding."

Grandpa Dominic gave me a startled look. Then he dropped the cigar butt into a glass of water on the oak table, twice licking the burn on the tip of his thumb.

"Do you read a lot?" he asked.

Oh yes, I said. I told him we had so many books at home that some had to be taken by Father to the health centre, and quite a few had been shifted up to the loft of our house. I read indiscriminately, often taking books off the shelves with eyes closed. But I never read any quite to the end. I flipped through books, reading only the bits that engaged my interest for whatever reason. Perhaps I had read too much or too many different things, for everything now seemed to be jumbled up in a strange mess in which I often got lost.

"I bet you do," said Grandpa Dominic.

He took another cigar from the box, but did not light it immediately. Staring out the window, he kept tapping with it against the table until the bottom end began to fray and bits of tobacco came off. Finally he pushed it between his teeth.

"And what are you reading now?" he muttered as he struck a match.

I said I was reading a book which was in fact being read by Father, which meant that I was reading it only when he was at work. The book was *Dream-analysis in its Practical Application,* written by somebody called Carl Gustav Jung. I had found it on Father's bedside table by chance as I passed the bedroom with the door ajar, and was attracted by its blue cover.

"Interesting reading?" asked Grandpa Dominic.

I said it was a difficult book to read, with long, complicated sentences, so I wasn't reading all of it but only the bits underlined by Father. Some of those passages I did not understand either, but at least I knew why Father was reading the book: to get additional information on the subject of dreams, prior to his attempt to wrestle me from their destructive power, as he had put it.

"Do you read this book every day?"

I admitted that actually I was no longer reading it. Father had taken it to his surgery, where he read it whenever he managed to snatch a moment of time, and where he kept it locked away in his desk. He must have realised that I was reading the underlined passages, and felt that the book would increase my confusion. After all my problems had started with books; I had read too much and understood too little.

"But I've copied some of the underlined sentences," I said, producing a folded sheet from my pocket. "Including those words I said earlier."

Grandpa Dominic seemed relieved. "Yes, I was hoping they weren't yours."

I unfolded the sheet and read: "We must never forget in dream-analysis, even for a moment, that we move on treacherous ground where nothing is certain but uncertainty. A suitable warning to the dream-interpreter – if only it were not so paradoxical – would be: Do anything you like, only don't try to understand."

"Interesting," was grandpa's comment.

"Why then should we question the importance of unconscious happenings?" I carried on. "Dreams give information about the secrets of the inner life and reveal to the dreamer the hidden factors of his personality. As long as these are undiscovered, they disturb his waking life and betray themselves only in the form of symptoms."

"Probably true," agreed Grandpa Dominic, who had completely forgotten he was holding a burning cigar in his hand. "Have you much more of this?"

I nodded.

"Read me one more, and the rest we should leave for some other time, don't you think?"

"I'll read one that's slightly longer," I said by way of apology. I waited for grandpa to nod his assent before I continued.

"But if his relation to his Father is really excellent, why must the dream manufacture such an improbable story to discredit the father? The dreamer's unconscious must have a distinct tendency to produce such a dream. Does the young man have resistances to his father, after all, which are perhaps fed by jealousy or a certain sense of inferiority? The answer, in this case, would be that his unconscious clearly tries to depreciate his father. If we take this as compensation, we are forced to the conclusion that his relation to his father is not only good but too good. His father is still too much the guarantor of his existence, and he is still living what I call a provisional life. He runs the risk of failing to realise himself because there is too much 'father' on every side. This is why the unconscious manufactures a kind of blasphemy: it seeks to lower the father and to elevate the son."

I folded the sheet and pushed it back into my pocket. Grandpa Dominic was completely enveloped in smoke. Finally, as he was about to start coughing, he pulled the cigar from his mouth and blew the smoke away. But he was too late to avoid a fit of coughing anyway.

"And what do you think about this?" he asked when he regained his calm.

"I don't know," I said. "I trust my father. He always knows what he is doing. He'll do whatever is best for me."

"Yes, he probably does know what he's doing," grandpa said with an edge to his voice. "Very clever, your father. When will this dreaming together, as he calls it, take place?"

"Tomorrow," I said. "Tomorrow is Sunday and Mother will be away."

"She isn't supposed to know?"

"She wouldn't understand. She understands very little."

"Well," he said after a while as he started to rise from the arm-chair, "make sure your father doesn't lose you in the dream he wants to dream with you. It just wouldn't do, being lost in a dream forever, would it? Not for a boy of your age anyway. It wouldn't matter for me, but I've lived my life. Yours is before you. Promise you'll be careful."

"Sure," I said.

"Let me show you to the door."

The next day Mother got up very early, climbed on her bicycle and pedalled off to one of the neighbouring villages to spend the day with Aunt Yolanda. She said she would be back rather late, so we should get some lunch at the village inn. Yes, Father said, yes, we will, don't you worry about us. As soon as she disappeared behind the trees, he rubbed his hands together and winked at me. "Ready?"

Not knowing what to say, I vaguely nodded.

Father said I should enter our common dream first. He would follow as soon as he found it convenient. He would stay at my side, waiting for the best opportunity to intervene. He did not elaborate on what he meant by that, he simply said that I should take a bath, comb my hair and put on my Sunday clothes. Dreams are like a journey into the unknown, where there is no way of knowing who you are going to meet. "Suppose we run into a pretty girl who'll take a fancy to you? What sort of impression do you think you'd make in your filthy tracksuit?"

When I was dressed, he asked me to sit in the big armchair in the living room and wait for the dream to begin. It would begin as soon as I became aware of flames in the fireplace. From then on nothing would be real any more; everything would be a dream.

I mentioned that we were in the middle of summer. I would have to wait a long time for a fire to start in the fireplace. Father rapped me on the head with his knuckles and said that by the time I noticed flames I would already be in the dream world, where seasons do not follow one another in the same way.

He produced a pocket watch on a silver chain and dangled it in front of my eyes. I followed the movements of the watch until my eyes began to close and heavy tiredness began to sweep over me. Suddenly both Father and the watch dissolved. I found myself sitting next to the fireplace, trying to read a book. Logs in the fireplace were being consumed by crackling flames. Unable to concentrate on reading, I stared into the flames as if trying to pour all my tiredness into them. But tiredness grew, and eventually I became very light-headed. My body swayed and swivelled until it regained a precarious balance, a kind of hovering. Maybe I was sitting too close to the fire. But as soon as I thought that my unusual sensations might be caused by heat I started to shiver. An icy cold began to climb from my feet toward my knees, where it stopped.

It felt as if my body had poured all its weight into the lower half of my legs. When eventually the feeling of cold began to rise again, travelling towards my groin, it felt as if I were growing out of my legs into some kind of new, unfamiliar shape. The cold reached my penis and slid into it. My penis swelled as if trying to burst; it felt like a wild animal, attacking me.

Then I heard the crackle of the flames again, and felt the heat returning, and the cold draining away. The attack of the penis was over, unexplained, inexplicable, leaving a bitter-sweet taste in my mouth. Next I heard a car pull up in front of the house. I moved to the window and looked out. Sitting behind the wheel was a middle-aged, read-bearded gentleman of slow, careful movements, with a worried expression on his face. He switched the engine off, but remained sitting in the car for another minute. Then, still with an air of indecision about him, he opened the door and climbed out. He was wearing a black beret, and had a silk shawl wrapped round his neck.

Who could this be? He walked slowly toward the entrance. He rang the bell. As I opened the door I came face to face with Father! I could not have sworn that it was him; it could easily have been someone who just reminded me of him. The man's eyes were after all mistier, less alive than my father's. But something in his bearing and expression was telling me that this couldn't possibly be anyone else; I even recognized his voice as he smiled at me and said, "Shall we go?"

He turned and walked back to the car. The car was definitely Father's, together with the dented door on the driver's side and the cracked rear indicator light. And as I climbed into the seat next to him, he swerved away from the house and onto the road with Father's usual tenacity, as if claiming priority for himself.

"Is that you?" I asked him.

He said that we were both only dream images now, with uncertain and possibly overlapping identities. "But that's not important," he added. "We're on our way. Everything we see, hear and smell is a dream. Everything's happening, but nothing is real. Isn't that nice?"

11

After a while everything around me turns soft and elusive, as if present and absent simultaneously, including the countryside opening up before us. It's a beautiful day, we're in the middle of summer again; the hills are bathed in sunlight. In one of the villages we are joined by a friend of Father's, a building engineer, who then continuously grumbles about the weather, world, life, women, government. The road descends into the heart of a thick wood. Father parks in a lay-by and we walk among the trees looking for mushrooms. According to the engineer, they should be growing there "like mushrooms after the rain". But we fail to find any – because "we're blind", the engineer says. Then they shoot with an old pistol. They refuse to let me try.

"You're still a virgin," the engineer slaps me on the back in a manner I find much too familiar. "First you have to aim at a soft target."

I feign indifference, saying little.

We climb back in the car and drive on, leaving the wood behind. Late mist seems to be descending on the surrounding fields. The world looks bluish and empty. The road we are on leads to the city. In one of the villages, crossing a bridge over a stream, we notice two girls. They are leaning against the bridge railing. One is tall and blond, the other smaller, plumper, with jet-black hair, maybe a Gypsy.

The engineer looks at his wrist-watch and says, "Right on time."

Father slams on the brakes, all three of us are thrown forward, then back against the seats. Father changes gears, slowly reverses and stops on the bridge. The girls smile. The blond one is pretty like a girl from a magazine.

"Which one do you like best?" the engineer peers at me from the front seat.

Father says, "Adam, answer the gentleman."

I say nothing. I just look. To be honest, I like both of them, but the black one a little less. A lot less. To be honest, I only like the blond one. But they're both taller than I am; at fourteen, I am smaller than most boys of my age.

The engineer beckons to them, and they come across the road. They climb in at the back, next to me. Helen, the blond one, sits in the middle. I sit on her right. They don't look like girls from a farm. The dark one admits that she has two children. I try to imagine what they might look like. I decide I don't like them. Actually it is their mother I'm not really fond of. She has too much make-up on her face. And there is something sneaky about the way she looks at me. To be honest, there is only one girl I like, and that's Eve. But she does not feature in this particular dream.

The blond girl starts to talk. She is answering the engineer's questions. Yes, she is employed; she works in a clothing factory. But she earns very little. Her boyfriend had left her, she cut her wrist, but the neighbour found her and she was saved. Her present boyfriend is in jail for stealing cars. But her colleague, sitting next to her, has got it worked out much better. She lives by giving men what they want. Not the sort of thing she herself would like to do all the time.

"Come on," the black one croaks with an unpleasant voice, "next you'll say you're a virgin."

"Well," says Helen bitchily, "compared to you I almost am."

I can hear the dark one sharply drawing in air. But that's where it stops, nothing is said, the girls manage to avoid a fight.

The engineer turns around and asks, "Adam, do you know what these girls are talking about?"

"Of course he does," Father steps in and saves me from trying to think of an answer. I stare out of the window, wondering why we are taking the girls with us, and where. But since it's only a dream, guided by Father who knows what he is doing, I feel safe, nothing bad can happen to me. I do feel uncomfortable, but I'm not afraid. I distinctly remember having fallen asleep in the chair at home, and I believe that that's where I will wake up. Father, obviously reading my thoughts, confirms this by winking at me.

"We're nearly there," he says as we reach the outskirts of the city.

I cannot imagine where this should be, but the others seem to know quite well, even the girls. The black one points to the left and says, "Down there, by the river."

She is right: on the bank of the dull-brown, lazy river, close to the stone bridge which is spanning it, there is an exhibition of agricultural tools and machines, a fair combined with a circus. Father parks the car in one of the back streets and we push our way into the crowd. I don't think I have ever seen so many people in one place. They eat grilled sausages and fat pieces of pork, wash it all down with kegs of frothy beer, queue for the merry-go-round, the bowling alley, the house of horrors, the shooting gallery, even for room on the raised dance floor, where strange looking people move around to the tune of a very strange sounding folk music.

"Well, how do you like our common dream?" Father asks, squeezing my shoulders.

I merely shrug. I dare not tell him that not very much. But Father can see that I'm tired of all the jostling and shouting.

"Not to worry," he says. "Dreams can be speeded up."

We join the engineer and the two girls who are drinking beer at a round wooden table. The engineer has white froth on his moustaches. He had just counted a number of banknotes on the table. In front of the beady eyes of the dark one, Helen counts them once more, rolls them into a spool which she fastens with a rubber band, and puts them into her handbag. I have never seen girls drinking beer before. I can tell from the ease with which they sip it from the tall glasses that this isn't their first time.

"What about you two?" Helen looks at the engineer, and then at Father.

"Some other time," the engineer looks at me. "Youth must be first." His heavy hand lands crushingly on my shoulder. "Right, boy?"

I have no idea what all this could mean, but I'm not bothered; in dreams things are often confused, leading nowhere. As evening approaches and mist begins to envelop the river as well, we make our way back to the car. Soon we are returning along the road which brought us to the city. We are sitting in the same way as before, the only difference being that Helen is now almost squeezed against me, I can feel the whole length of her slim, firm thigh pressed against mine. Every now and then she gives me a curious and perhaps slightly sneering look. In a smallish town perched on top of a hill Father brings the car to a halt in front of an inn. We climb out and choose one of the empty tables in the garden. The men order beer. The girls, for a change, demand a bottle of the best wine. I drink apple juice. Father wants to know if I am hungry. I shake my head.

The hills are slowly disappearing in the evening mist. From the valley below, darkness is stealthily moving up the slopes, dissolving the shapes of trees, houses, vineyards and fields into a world of ill-defined shadows. The men leave the table and drive off in the car. "Don't worry," the engineer shouts through the car window just before they disappear. "Trust the girls, they have plenty of experience."

Left alone, we sit at the table and look at the procession of shadows moving up from the valley. I wish that this dream would soon end. I make an effort to wake up, but then I relax. I remember Father; I don't want to leave him alone in the dream. We must emerge from it together, in the same way we sank into it. But the purpose of the dream is no clearer to me now than it was at the beginning.

The girls drink wine. We are alone in the garden. Helen leans over into my lap and asks me to kiss her and caress her legs. But she is wearing course linen trousers. I feel no skin as I glide my hand along her left thigh. And her lips are cold, unresponsive. The grass is already covered with evening dew. Lights come on inside the inn. The girls persuade me to drink a glass of wine. My brain relaxes; my body feels a pleasant warmth. I begin to talk. First about my little brother, who lives in a bottle. And how he cannot open his mouth, because he floats in a liquid. How he transmits his thoughts to me through his eyes. Then I mention how we are really in the middle of winter because as Father and I left the house there were flames in the fire-place. I was hot. And it must have been because of the heat that my penis attacked me.

The girls, who have listened attentively, exchange glances. Finally Helen says, "Are you being treated for this?"

I tell them that I'm being treated by Father, who is a doctor, the best in the world. He was brave enough to accompany me into the dream we are now dreaming together. What other doctor would have done that? Everything that is happening now is a dream; nothing of what we see, hear, or smell is real.

"Oh you poor boy," says Helen and gently strokes my hair.

The mist is now all around us, I can feel it on my cheeks; it is cold. The church clock delivers eleven strikes. There is no sign of Father. They are closing the inn, we have to leave. Like shadows we slink off along the road leading into the centre of the town. It's a very small town, almost a village. I am tired and sleepy. I am beginning to worry that Father might not return. Where will I sleep? It's a strange thought, asking oneself where one will sleep in a dream, but the night is cold and my worry is almost real. We roam around, passing houses, shuttered shops, and silent buildings. The church clock announces the time: half past midnight. And still there is no sign of Father.

Finally the dark-haired girl makes a suggestion. She will sleep in Helen's room, where we can't go because the neighbour hears every sound. Helen and I can go up the hill to her house. Just before daybreak they will swap again, and I will no doubt be picked up by Father. But the blond beauty rejects the suggestion out of hand. That is not possible, she says, she simply has to sleep in her room.

"Besides, the boy's in such a state that I couldn't do this," she adds in a whisper.

"We shouldn't have taken the money," says the dark girl.

We stand in the middle of the road, silent, shivering. No one seems to know what to do. I feel that the girls probably hate me. I wish I could just leave them and walk off, and follow the road all the way home. But that would take me at least seven hours. And I might miss Father, who is no doubt returning to pick me up.

There must be a reason for his running late. I am stuck, I have to wait. In the end the black girl invites me to go with her and sleep at her place, if there is no other way, and if I want to.

Yes, it's okay, I nod. She and Helen move away a few steps and engage in a brief conversation, gesticulating. Because of my "hypertrophy of the senses" my ears pick up their every word. They argue about the money Helen received from the engineer. The dark-haired girl wants to have it. Helen insists that it was for both of them, and she will give her no more than half.

"Then do half of what you got the money for!" the dark girl snaps back.

"You won't have to do your half either," Helen says. "Can't you see he is sick in the head? Some Father, I must say, leaving him to the likes of us."

She walks off and disappears in the night.

I follow the black-haired girl up the road. She keeps explaining that her room is very simple, and I shouldn't be shocked. As a doctor's son I must be used to better things. I'm only half listening. I just want to spend the night somewhere, anywhere, as long as I won't be cold. We reach a half-ruined old house at the top of the hill, the last in the row. That's where she lives. Sharing with an old woman, who sleeps next door. We enter a very dark room. She moves around as if looking for something. Finally she lights a battered petroleum lamp. I had never been in a house without electricity. There is a horrible smell. I feel dizzy and faint, partly, no doubt, because of the wine. The furniture is half-rotten and old. There are cobwebs on the walls. The wooden floor is full of dust. Vile-smelling clothes are strewn all over the place.

"Will you sleep next to me?" she asks, almost shyly.

Why ever not, I think to myself and start removing my clothes. The woman blows out the lamp and climbs into the bed. I climb in next to her. I hear banging noises inside my skull. I fear that the overpowering smell will prevent me from sleeping. But under the blanket I gradually begin to warm up, and the smell becomes less offensive. I can feel the woman's hand moving and reaching toward me. Softly yet firmly she takes hold of my right hand and places it on her thigh. Still holding it, she slides it slowly towards the knee, and then slowly back towards the groin. The thigh is well-rounded, almost fat. Different from Eve's, which is slim, firm and girlish.

"Tell me more about that attack," the woman says from under the blanket. "You said you were attacked by your penis."

I remain silent. That is the last thing I want to talk about, especially at this moment. She turns towards me. As she does so she lifts the blanket a little. My nostrils get the full blast of the foulest smell I have ever encountered, composed of an unwashed body, old sweat, deodorant defeated by what it was meant to disguise, and of something faintly acid and sour.

"Menstruation," she breathes into my ear. Her wine-laden breath licks my ear-drum like a hot tongue. "It's almost finished. It should be okay."

The feeling of faintness grows and I lie there hovering on the edge of consciousness. In the beam of the street-light shining in through the window I see primordial monsters dancing around the bed. I close my eyes and pretend to be asleep. Under the blanket her hand is on the move once again, slithering like a snake towards my navel, where it pauses, throbbing with heat. Then it moves on towards my underpants, burrows its way inside, takes hold of my flaccid penis, pulls it out and begins to rub it.

I pretend that the penis doesn't belong to me. That I'm not I. That I had wandered into this dream by mistake, while Father is, probably in despair, looking for me in another dream, the one we had entered together.

"Father," I pray in my thoughts, "Father, come and take me away."

The five-tongued snake slithers away and leaves me alone.

In despair I begin to hope it is possible to fall asleep inside a dream while actually dreaming it, and in that sleep switch to another, pleasanter dream. I surrender to the weight of exhaustion. It works: soon I begin to float across an invisible boundary into what looks like a completely new dream. I look around to find Father. But all I see are black, fast moving clouds trembling with flashes of lightning. Suddenly I hear the sound of a raging wind. As the storm approaches, a familiar unpleasant feeling sweeps over me: as if I were experiencing another attack of the penis. As it swells and begins to hurt, it is suddenly, with a single violent move, engorged by a damp, warm mouth which greedily begins to chew and swallow it. Something untidy and gasping sways above me, the head of a monster. I, too, struggle for air, my heart pounds as if trying to leap from my chest, I feel like vomiting. My penis has been attacked by a snake which is trying, with rough thrusting movements, to swallow it and digest it with its evil-smelling juices.

Finally the twitching monster above me stops, for a brief moment freezes and then shivers above me, emitting low moans for what seems like eternity. Then it moves away and collapses next to me, breathing heavily. My nostrils register a huge mound of rumpled sweaty hair. The room is spinning. I can hear thunder rumbling in the distance, there is a flash of lightning, followed by a gush of wind which rattles the window panes. I am back in the dream I tried to escape. Now I'm afraid of falling asleep again. I lie on the hard wooden frame of the bed to remain awake in a dream from which a little earlier I had sunk into the most horrible nightmare, worse than any I could ever imagine.

The storm is drawing closer. The street-lamp outside sways in the wind, and the stripes from its light quiver on the wall of the room. Wafting towards me from the body lying next to me is a vile mixture of smells. I remember that the body belongs to the black-haired girl who had brought me to the old house. I, too, smell unpleasantly: of her body, her blood, her perspiration. I would like to run away and jump head first into clear, cleansing water.

I sink into a thick haze again, hovering on the edge of consciousness. I feel betrayed; Father had taken me into a dream and then left me there without guidance. At the first sign of dawn I jump out of bed, dress in a record time, grab my shoes and stagger out into the light of the coming day. I run through the morning mist, bare feet landing on the still dewy surface of the asphalt, past the houses which lean after me like gaping carnivores smelling their first morning prey, along the road which snakes its way out of the town and toward open fields. After running for ten minutes, I see headlights emerge from the mist.

"Why didn't you wait for me at the inn?" I hear Father's angry voice.

12

At the beginning of September, a few days before the start of the new school year, Eve returned to her parents in town. I had hoped she would come and say good-bye to me, but she didn't; her Father, a stiff-backed gentleman in a dark suit, drove her away in a black Mercedes. She never said good-bye to Father, either – except in my dream, during which I saw them among the bushes behind the health centre. She held him tightly and cried, and he kept stroking her hair. Then they kissed for a long time. It seemed to me that Father, too, had tears in his eyes. This was the first time I realised that Father actually suffered in my dreams, and for the first time I sincerely wished that they would come to an end, or that Father would cure me of this extraordinary affliction. Or, if he couldn't, that someone else would, even, in the absence of anyone nicer, Dr Kleindienst. The unpleasant dream in which Father joined me and then abandoned me had, perhaps not surprisingly, failed to achieve its aim.

Following Eve's departure I was assaulted by persistent images of water, which filled my mind like a sudden infusion I couldn't get rid of. All objects, sounds and smells pointed my attention in the direction of the squishy liquid within me. The water was turbulent, coursing through my inner landscape day and night. Occasionally it resembled a large stagnant pool reaching all the way to the horizon, coming alive only if an invisible frog stirred the surface from below, or a drop of moisture fell into it from the leaves of a tree above it. Although I kept pushing the thought away, it was more obvious every day that I was missing something, and that the feeling within me was one of longing: for something lost, for something that had become a part of me and now seemed to be gone forever.

The feeling was reinforced during the first day at school when we had to write a free composition on the subject of "What happened to me during summer holidays". While navigating the waters of memory I couldn't help feeling a sense of superiority with regard to my fellow pupils, whose summer months must have been boring beyond belief. As I saw them labouring over their exercise-books I felt a surge of pride at the thought that my summer had been so different, so exceptional, and so mysterious when compared to their boring lives. So deeply was I sucked into the memory of past events that I didn't even realise I had started to write, and when I finally did I couldn't tell whether I was recording memories or a dream unfolding there and then. That it was a dream became obvious when I suddenly noticed Eve coming towards me across a meadow. I expected to see Father next, but he refused to turn up, Eve was coming alone, straight toward me. It was like watching a film I had seen before, but reshot on a different location and modified.

As she came up to me she took my hand and gently placed it on her abdomen. "I'm going to be a Mummy," she said. She pulled me along with her, and the next moment we were in the waiting room of the health centre, with Father standing in the doorway of his surgery as if expecting us. He put his arm around Eve's waist and lifted her onto the examining table. She was naked. It was only now that I saw her hugely swollen belly. She pulled up her legs and opened them wide. Father put a plastic glove on his hand and reached deep inside her, rummaging around as if looking for something. Eve lay without moving, with her eyes fixed at the ceiling.

"It doesn't look good," Father said as he pulled out his hand. He walked to the window and stared at the trees outside. I felt a wave of anxiety. When Father spoke his voice had a gloating edge to it. "Your brother has a frog's head," he said. I failed to understand what he was trying to tell me. He turned around and said, "Your little brother will be born with the head of a frog, he will have bulging eyes, and he'll keep blinking with them!" I could feel the ground parting under my feet. "That's impossible," I said.

Still, Father continued in a cold voice, that's of no importance, I just had to imagine that there is no child, that there never was one and never will be. "But there is a child," I objected, "the child must be born." "Don't be ridiculous," Father said. "Do you want a brother with a frog's head, so that people will point at you? We shall put him in a glass jar and hide him in the cellar, for possible scientific research later on. We shall stick a label on the jar, write Abortus on it, and that'll be that."

There followed a jump to our house, where Abortus was already padding around, aged three. Mother cooked for him, washed him and took care of his other needs. Father and Eve were no longer there. "We don't need anybody," Mother kept saying. "The main thing is that you have a brother, someone to talk to." But I couldn't talk to Abortus, because he couldn't speak. What took me longest to get used to were his tiny eyes, with which he never stopped blinking, just like a frog. When he cried he opened his already wide mouth even wider, and it seemed that his entire head consisted of no more than his mouth, with slight folds of skin where his ears should have been. His voice was unpleasantly shrill and squawking, just like a frog's, but the only time we heard it was when he cried, which he did very rarely. He was a well-behaved frog-boy, very accommodating and understanding, not at all obdurate or frivolous. In fact, very often he gave the impression of being more a humble, loyal pet than a human being.

What I found strange was that he did not care for toys. Mother and I bought him various dolls, stuffed animals, tin soldiers, squeaking clocks, cars, clattering monkeys, but nothing held his attention for longer than the first polite moment, after which he quietly put each new offer on the floor and stared at his feet as if unhappy that he was unable to please us. I pulled a chair to the window and lifted him onto it. As long as he could look out at the orchard, the hedge, the road, the fields, the woods and the church on top of the hill he was happy. He looked at everything with a mixture of surprised curiosity and thoughtful wonder.

One day he picked up a book and started to read. It was Jung's *Dream-analysis in its Application*. He read it with ease and great interest, as if he had been taught reading years ago and had read thousands of books. When he came to the last page he wanted more, so I took him up to Father's library, where he settled down happily with a pile of books picked at random off the nearest shelves. It was from books that he learned about the wonders of the world outside, just as I had done before him. Then, one day, he suddenly uttered his first words, still hesitant, but clear in intention: he asked to be taken out, to see people, woods, rivers, hills, and to feel the wind on his skin.

Next we were crossing a grassy meadow on our way to the village behind the woods. I had never seen Abortus so happy; he squawked and shouted and squealed and grunted with joy. He couldn't keep still; he ran this way and that and hopped about, half the time on all fours, very much like a frog. As we reached a small pond I nearly died as I saw him plunge into it and splash about in the water, half the time below the surface. When finally he crawled out he grunted with pleasure. There were frogs in the pond, one of them sitting on a floating oak leaf. He kept looking at it for a long time without blinking. As we continued on our way he seemed tired, lost in thoughts, depressed.

But again he came alive. As we were crossing the fields he suddenly turned to me with a series of questions. Why does the wheat grow? Where does the wind come from? Why don't people build houses under the ground? Because then, when they died, they wouldn't have to be buried, he said, they could just stay at home. And then, suddenly: Who is my Father? Who is my Mother? Who am I? Why aren't apple trees bigger than oak trees? Why are some trees straight and others bent? As we came out of the wood his body began to resemble a walking question-mark.

We came to the village inn, where they knew me well, because whenever Mother didn't feel like cooking, Father and I had to go there for lunch or dinner. We sat down at an empty table and waited to be served. People stared at Abortus as if transfixed. A woman at the table next to ours started to vomit; then she fainted and had to be carried out. Others followed her, leaving their tables with meals unfinished. Soon the place was empty except for the waiters, Abortus and me. Eventually we were approached by a thick-set man in a dark shirt, the inn-keeper. He tried very hard to keep his eyes off Abortus. It's like this, he said. We are kindly requested to leave the inn. No two ways about it.

I said that we came to the inn as guests, just like any other guest, all we want is an orange juice each, we are thirsty, and we find the attitude of the serving staff humiliating, to say the least. We demand an apology. The inn-keeper said that he understood my sentiments and sympathised with them, but unfortunately he couldn't help me; at the end of the day he had to think of himself and his employees. If we're not willing to meet him halfway and leave, he will have no choice but to call the police who will not shilly-shally but will do what is expected of them. The blame for whatever might happen will be mine and mine alone, because of my stubbornness and defiance.

I repeated that we were guests, and wanted no more than what guests are entitled to: basic respect and whatever they order, in our case two orange juices. The inn-keeper withdrew. Within minutes the village cop approached us. He leaned on the table with both hands and breathed at me: You're kindly requested to get out of here. For a brief moment his eyes wandered toward Abortus, who was innocently admiring his uniform. The policeman winced and grew pale, but he managed to pull himself together and give me a look which meant only one thing: get out or else. I began to explain that we wanted no more than two orange juices, which was hardly against the law, but he cut me short and said: boy, I'm warning you, if you don't get out of here I'll have no choice but to use force.

I remained cool. I insisted that my brother and I would not leave the inn until we were served. The policeman gave me a glassy look which faded into a vacant stare. The next moment he grabbed Abortus and ran with him to the door. He tossed him into the courtyard as if getting rid of a vile snake. Abortus landed on his head and lost consciousness. I ran to help him but the policeman hit me on the head with his truncheon. The last thing I remembered was sinking into a dark abyss.

"Adam," I heard the teacher's voice, "have you finished?"

"I don't know," I said. "I don't know how this should end."

"Well, it's ending here," said the teacher. "Because everyone else finished five minutes ago. Would you please come forward and read your composition to the class?"

"No," I said. "This is a dream. I don't share dreams with other people. Only with my little brother."

The teacher snatched the exercise book from my hands and walked with it to the front of the classroom. "You'll have to share it with me and the rest of the class," he said. "And then I may decide to share it with your Father. Sharing is good. It tells us who we are, what we're about. Cathy, will you come and read Adam's composition to us?"

I grabbed my bag and ran to the door.

I ran to the end of the corridor, down the stairs, taking three at a time, then across the courtyard, and finally across the fields along the shortest route to the health centre. I was making longer leaps than ever, driven by a strange foreboding that something had happened to Abortus; I had not been to the basement for some time.

My first thought as I slid down the chute was that I would I never see him again. But there he was, floating in his glass jar as if completely unaware of what we had just gone through in my dream. His expression seemed more peaceful than ever; almost as though he were grateful for being condemned to live inside a glass jar, protected from the turbulence of the outside world. I reached past the jar to get at my dream diary and write down my latest dream, if only because it differed so markedly from all the others.

But as I did so I noticed a change in my brother's eyes. They seemed to have clouded over and become withdrawn. That was his way of expressing a wish. My way of reading his wishes was trying to guess what he might have meant. It seemed to me that he would be happier if I did not record my latest dream. He would prefer not to learn what would have happened to him if he had grown into a little boy. I respected his wishes, so I said nothing, not a word. That was the best, the only way of protecting him. The main thing was that he was still there, safe inside his little home.

13

But my urge to talk to someone about the event at school was so great that I didn't go home. I ran along hidden footpaths up the hill until I reached Grandpa Dominic's house. At first it seemed that he wasn't at home. The door was unlocked, but the dark, cluttered, slightly malodorous rooms were filled with an air of late-summer solitude. The sun rays penetrated the clusters of tree branches and shone through the gaps in the drawn curtains in the same way as during my first visit, resting on walls, floors and pieces of furniture in the shape of rhomboids, squares and strangely reclining animals.

A strange force made me hurry up the stairs to the first floor, and to the end of the corridor, until I found myself in Eve's room. I went down on my knees. I buried my face in the blanket which covered the bed. I breathed in the smell of dusty old wool and, I could have sworn, barely perceptible traces of sweet feminine scents. I reached under the bed, half hoping to find the plastic bag with Eve's snaps. Of course it wasn't there.

I stayed in her room for a long time, feeding on memories. When eventually I wandered back down the corridor it was with a burning feeling of emptiness in my heart. I felt that I would never see her again, neither in dreams nor for real. It occurred to me that she may not have been real at all, but merely a phantom, born out of the summer solitude. I paused in the living room where half the African gods were basking in the sun shining in through the window. The other half stood in deep shadow, barely visible. I watched their white painted eyes, wondering what secret powers lay behind them. Would they be able to...

"Please bring her back," I whispered. "Make her real."

A floorboard creaked somewhere behind me. I turned, but there was no one there. Then I felt the weight of a large hand on my shoulder. It gripped me gently and turned me around. It was Grandpa Dominic.

"You mustn't tell them everything," he said. "They might turn things against you. They feed on human energy, you see? They hope to collect enough of it to fly back to Africa. I should've left them where I found them. Believing that they would protect me in my old age was a dream of a much younger man. Dreams of young men, especially very young men, rarely ensure a happy old age. Come with me."

I followed him out into the courtyard and round the corner of the house into the orchard. We passed a pool of dark-green water, fringed by twisted brambles and long stalks of sorrel.

"Don't look at that water," said Grandpa Dominic. "I hate it." We carried on to a large apple tree and sat down on the blanket he had spread in its shade.

"I've been reading old diaries," he said, pointing to three large voluminous exercise-books half hidden in the tall grass next to the blanket. "You wouldn't believe how much life there is on those pages. More than in ten surrounding villages! You should write a diary, too."

It was like always when I was with Grandpa Dominic: it was either the expression in his eyes, or an encouraging gesture, but the floodgates in me suddenly yielded and I started to pour out things I would never tell anyone else, even things I never realised were bothering me. I told him that I was already onto my second diary, *Dreams II,* and that I had recorded in detail all my dreams, especially those involving Father and Eve. I told him about Father's basement and his experiments, and about my little brother Abortus. I told him about the dream that Father and I dreamed together, and which was supposed to cure me. Finally I told him about the one dream I decided not to record in the diary, partly because of Abortus and partly because I had already written it down at school, as a free composition entitled "What happened to me during summer holidays". I also told him about my fear that the teacher would show the piece to my Father.

Grandpa Dominic listened as intently as ever, almost as though he were hard of hearing. He looked very serious, but every now and then he would nod and give me an encouraging smile. He never looked me in the eyes; he was busy with the cigar which he took from his box, nervously twisting it in his fingers. He did not light it; he waited for the torrent of my words to abate.

"And those others dreams," he finally asked, reaching for the box of matches, "about Father and Eve, are you still having them?" He shielded the match with his hand, so that the light breeze which rustled the leaves above us wouldn't extinguish the flame.

I said that obviously I had been cured of those dreams. The last one I had was on the day of Eve's departure, when I dreamed about her and Father saying good-bye to each other in the bushes behind the health centre. Since then there's been nothing. It must have been the delayed effect of the dream in which my Father joined me that finally cured me, just as Father had predicted.

"Are you sure of that?" Grandpa Dominic suddenly spoke in a tone he had not used before, almost with a touch of impatience and anger. "Suppose you're having these dreams only when Eve is here? Maybe we should try to find out. What do you think? Dreams like that shouldn't be taken lightly."

He looked at me, but I merely shrugged, not knowing what to say.

"Shall I ask her to come for a weekend?"

"Yes please," I breathed, avoiding his eyes.

She came four days later. It was Saturday. My dreams returned the same day, about midday, just as I had slid down the chute into the basement to say hello to Abortus. Suddenly I heard a key in the door. I climbed behind a dusty chest of drawers which was full of out-of-date medicines. There wasn't much room, I was wedged between the drawer and a damp wall, and there were cobwebs everywhere. But it was dark in that part of the basement, no one would see me.

As the door squealed open, Father entered first. Then he stepped back to let Eve follow him in. He closed the door and bolted it. He was wearing a white coat; he must have come straight from the surgery. Eve was in jeans, the first time she wasn't wearing a skirt.

She seemed to have lost so much weight that the jeans kept sliding off her hips, and she kept pulling them up. In the beam of light coming in through the window her face looked gaunt and exhausted, with black rings under her eyes.

She paused in front of Abortus and exclaimed: "What stuff did you give me this time? Something awfully good. I can see things I could never imagine!"

Father put his forefinger across her lips. "Not so loud, there are people upstairs."

"Where did you bring me?" she wondered, looking at the shelves which were not in darkness. She stared at the jars containing an excised tumour, a severed thumb, an amputated penis.

"My God," she said, "you can't be normal."

"No," Father said, "you're normal. A perfectly normal fifteen-year old, doing perfectly normal things. Come on, I haven't got much time. Where is this door to hell you keep offering me?"

With a practised move, Eve pulled her jeans and panties off and let them curl around her feet. She bent forward, leaning against the wall with her hands.

"Sometimes you're really nice to me. But sometimes you treat me like a slut. And do you know what? I like it. I may decide to become one when I grow up. Thanks to you. Does that make you happy?"

"Shut up," said Father and stepped behind her. From his movements
I could tell that he was trying to enter her, but couldn't quite make it.

"Move your legs apart," he became impatient.

"I can't," she grew angry, "unless I step out of these stupid jeans. Since when have you had problems, you never had any before."

The next moment Father succeeded. She gasped and stifled a moan; the she relaxed and, paying no attention to Father's thrusting movements, looked around at the shelves, commenting on the contents of the jars. "I know what these are. They're embryos, aren't they? That's what we're like before we enter this beautiful world.

That's what will grow in my womb if you're not careful with that dick of yours. Will you then cut it out of me? Put it in a glass jar, like all these? I wouldn't be surprised if they were all yours."

"Shut up," Father panted, "this is science, you know nothing about it."

"If this is science I'm glad I failed my entrance exams for the grammar school. Very glad. Because I don't want to learn anything. I know too much already. Will you be much longer?"

"Don't you like it?" Father asked.

"Not in a place like this."

My dream ended as soon as the door of the cellar was pulled shut and locked from outside. The only thing I couldn't quite understand was how I could have fallen asleep in such an uncomfortable position, wedged in behind the chest of drawers so tightly that one of my legs had gone completely numb, while my knees grew so stiff that I needed some time before I could move normally.

But the dream was so vivid that I decided to record it at once, every little detail, every thrust of Father's body, every Eve's sigh or subdued moan, as well as her feigned indifference to what she was engaged in. It took me an hour to write it all down, and when I did I read bits of it to Abortus. Although everything took place in front of his eyes, he couldn't have seen anything, since it all happened in my dream. When I pushed the diary back behind the jar I thought I saw a grateful smile on his face. The dream must have been a great shock to him, but he obviously enjoyed it as much as I did.

Toward the evening I ran into Grandpa Dominic in the village shop, where Mother had sent me to fetch a carton of milk for Father's coffee.

"How are the dreams?" he asked me as we came out.

"They're back."

"I was afraid of that," he said, looking straight ahead. "Yes, I was *very* much afraid of that. Will you let me know when they stop again?"

I promised I would, but I never got the chance because the next day, quite unexpectedly, Mother finally managed to convince

Father that we badly needed a few restful days at the sea. She had been trying to talk him into this great adventure for over a year, claiming that not going on holiday for more than three years simply wasn't normal for a normal family. No, Father would always reply, it isn't normal, but it is normal for an abnormal family, which is what by all accounts we were. But his main excuse had always been that he was unable to find a replacement, someone reliable to look after his patients while he was away. That's why Mother and I were so surprised when suddenly he announced that a certain Dr. Nachtigal, longing for fresh country air, had decided to stand in for him for a week, and that we were leaving the following morning.

"What about Adam's school?" Mother asked, suddenly worried, although nearly fainting with excitement.

"Adam?" Father gave me a long searching look. "The author of mad compositions, the dreamer of salacious dreams?" I was gripped by a terrible fear that he would decide to leave me behind. Then he winked at me and said, "Adam will get chicken pox. I shall write him a note."

14

The next morning we drove to the seaside. But we soon regretted Father's sudden decision, for the events which began to take place immediately upon our arrival could hardly be thought of as usual for a seaside holiday. It started at the hotel: as soon as we filed through the door, the receptionist looked at us as if he'd seen a ghost. Quite evidently we had not made him happy with our arrival. But he was sitting behind the reception counter, so it was natural to assume that he would carry out his duties regardless of his personal feelings about the guests. Although we were somewhat taken aback by the man's reaction, Father quietly and without hesitation ordered a room.

"With a view of the sea," he added.

As we walked up the creaking stairs to the first floor, I looked at the wobbling movements of the receptionist's huge behind, which, because of a torn trouser pocket on his right hip, reminded me of a malicious, derisive grin. I suddenly felt that we shouldn't have come; in the rhythmic movements of the grinning pocket I felt a disguised reproach. Just then my nostrils were assaulted by a violent smell of naphthalene, so strong that I almost lost my balance. If Father, who walked behind me, had not caught me, I would have tumbled down the stairs and struck Mother, who made up the rear, and then both of us would have ended up at the bottom of the stairs with broken necks. I felt dizzy at the thought; I gripped the banister as hard as I could.

"Nice smell," Father quipped, but Mother said, "Oh shut up."

The receptionist turned around as if he had predicted the moment the smell would make me swoon. He gave me a brief scornful look. Then he transferred his gaze to Father and with a sticky voice explained that it wasn't his fault; the season had ended, there were no guests, the hotel had been put in mothballs.

"I don't remember anyone staying at the hotel at this time of year for more than ten years," he said before panting on.

"If that were so," I heard Father mutter behind me, "the hotel would have been closed a long time ago."

On the landing the receptionist produced a bunch of keys and unlocked the nearest door. As he opened it and waved us into the room, the smell of naphthalene wafted towards us with a double force. I felt sick at the thought that I would have to breathe it in for a week.

"You'll have to open the window," I heard the receptionist's unctuous voice, "for the smell to escape. But if it won't, there's nothing much you can do, it's the time of year when mothballs take over."

Suddenly Mother unloaded one of her silly remarks, for at certain decisive moments she simply couldn't help contributing something outrageously stupid and unhelpful: she said that the smell wasn't so bad, really, we would just have to put up with it! For her it was enough that we were at the sea, finally together at the sea, and for that she was prepared to sleep on the floor, in the loo even!

"Where is the sea?" Father asked as he parted the curtains.

We were staring at the steep wall of a towering grey rock. Oh, said the receptionist, the sea is on the other side, but there the rooms are much smaller, and the smell of mothballs ten times worse. What is more, the rooms had not been properly cleaned after the departure of the last group of tourists; but if we ourselves wanted to clean one we were welcome to it; if we could make do with a single bed, that is.

"No," Mother decided, "we shall stay here."

That was her second stupid remark. But it wasn't just her remark that drove me out of the room; it was the sickly smell, and Father's unusual indifference. I promised to wait for them outside. I knew very well what they would do. Mother would open our suitcases and travel bags, she would put every single thing that we brought with us into the most suitable place; then she would take a shower, change her clothes, comb her hair; and she would do all that with special eagerness, almost with love. I knew it would take at least an hour for her to conclude this ritualistic succession of moves which to me seemed so empty of meaning. Father, in the meantime, complaining of sudden bowel cramps, would lock himself in the loo, together with the newspaper he had bought for the purpose, as soon as we arrived.

I waited for them in front of the hotel, sitting on the stone wall, dangling my legs above the sea. It spread out before me like a tired body of stagnant water, grey and lifeless, weighed down by the flotsam of the summer months. There wasn't a sail in sight. The promenade was empty, most shops were closed. The general atmosphere became even more depressing when we had lunch in the large dining room. They gave us a table near the rear wall, so that the waiter, in order to reach us, had to cross the entire empty hall. That could have been a coincidence, but I soon realised that in the side wall not far from our table was an archway leading to the main corridor. Coming and going along this corridor were an incredible number of hotel's employees, far too many considering that we were the only guests: cooks, waiters, washer-women, chambermaids and the like. That, too, could have been a coincidence, for they seemed busy carrying things from one end to the other, but their openly curious glances were sufficient evidence that it was us they wanted to see: us, three belated tourists, extravagant fools worthy of scorn, which the passers-by did very little to hide.

My conjecture was confirmed when a terrible quarrel erupted in the kitchen. From the words that reached us it was just possible to make out that the waiters were fighting for the right to serve us. We must have appeared so strange that they all wanted to get the closest possible look at us. They obviously reached no agreement, because they kept coming in turn: one brought the cutlery, another the napkins, the third soup, the fourth potatoes, and so on. Mother thought that their unusual interest was no more than a sign of their hospitality, and, of course, our importance.

"Yes," Father said, "a country doctor, his ledger clerk wife, and their mentally deranged son, important guests indeed."

"Don't you ever say that again," Mother spluttered, nearly choking on a piece of roast potato. "If anyone, it is you who is deranged."

"I may well be," Father said. "I just hope you won't be surprised if I behave accordingly."

After lunch we went for a walk. We walked along the gently curving pebbly beach from one end to the other, only to turn and walk back the same way. The tired sea heaved against the shore like a restless swamp. The colour of the rocky hills behind the town was deathly grey, the rocks did not glisten, and even the sunlight was unusually pale. All this was deceptive, of course, I could feel very strongly that the seeming indifference was hiding scorn, even hatred, for every now and then it became obvious that the thick, exhausted sea was trying to swallow us. The tiny pebbles under our feet offered very uncertain support for our shoes, they kept sliding from underneath them, and it wasn't long before I felt that the earth, too, was trying to suck us into its lower depths.

There was an immense difference between this and the image of the resort I remembered from three years earlier. During our previous holiday it had been green, restless, throbbing with life. Observed from the lower end of the beach, it had seemed to resemble a large living being, dressed in the garish colours of foreign tourists who walked up and down the promenade, argued about the price of a donkey ride along the beach, thronged in front of kiosks, shouted, chatted and laughed, freely exposing large sunburned bellies. Everywhere one could feel the excited unease of shy children who had come to the sea for the first time and were staring with awe at its windy turbulence, and the giggly joy of young girls licking ice-cream, turning the pages of girlie magazines or smearing their bodies with sun lotion.

But now it was different. Now we were alone with the dull, threatening sea. A cold wind had begun to sweep across it. As we reached the first houses I heard the shrieking of gulls above us. But as I looked up I could see nothing, just an empty pale sky. My anxiety grew. All the signs pointed to imminent danger. I felt a sudden urge to ask Father to take us away from this town as soon as possible.

Near the hotel Mother suddenly developed an urge to eat bananas.

"Bananas?" Father couldn't believe it. "In this place? At this time of year?"

But Mother insisted; I should go to the market and get some, while she and Father would go to the room and take a little rest. I looked at Father. He shrugged and looked away. Then he walked towards the hotel like a huge obedient dog. Mother gave me some money and quickly followed him. I ran towards the centre of the town, knowing quite well that no one would be selling bananas in the middle of September, not in this little town, not in this unearthly atmosphere in which everything seemed so unusual and displaced. I knew that bananas were merely Mother's excuse for getting rid of me. But I felt a great surge of relief myself. The thought passed my mind that perhaps it was Mother who was the source of my feelings of impending doom.

I crossed and re-crossed the town from one end to the other, but there were no bananas; the few greengrocers who were open looked at me as if I had fallen on my head, and everywhere my departure was followed by laughter and snide remarks. As I walked back I felt that even houses were leaning after me and sneering, creaking with their doors. I didn't want to return to the hotel too early; I paused on the pier and looked at the sea. I decided to think everything over and come to some sort of decision.

Moored on both sides of the pier were fishing and sailing boats, creaking and rubbing against each other as they rose and fell with the undulating sea. Watching them without any particular thought I suddenly felt that someone was watching me. As I turned I saw, standing a few steps behind me, a gaunt man who was wearing a loose thin cape. His face, elderly but smooth, looked impassive, as if carved from a piece of marble. He wasn't looking at me but straight ahead. Then he began to close and open his eyes in rapid succession, as if irritated by a piece of dust behind his eyelid.

He stopped doing that as abruptly as he had begun. He turned his face towards me. His eyes looked as if made of glass, filled with hard, dim ice. He moved closer and without saying anything grabbed me by the sleeve of my shirt. His cape smelled of a mixture of mould and cheap after-shave. He looked me straight in the eyes and pulled me closer. With his other hand he pointed across the sea.

"Can you see it?" he asked in a deep, rumbling voice. "Can you see the island? You can't. And why not? Because it's the same colour as the sea and the sky. It blends in with them, it's invisible. But it's there, I tell you. I can take you there with my boat, would you like that?"

Without letting me answer he continued, and his voice gathered speed as if rolling downhill. "I'm a boatman, a fisherman. I ferry tourists to little coves. And the islands. Especially that one. No one lives there. You can swim naked, walk around, shout at the top of your voice, swear; whatever you want. Total freedom. Shall we say tomorrow morning?"

I opened my mouth to answer, I moved my tongue, but suddenly it occurred to me that I don't know what to say; the only thing that came out of my mouth was a strange, animal-like squawk. The man winced, let go of my sleeve and took a step back.

"Are you all right?" he asked, trying to sound concerned.

He moved closer and reached out to touch me again, but as he did so my right hand flew in the air and hit him in the face. It was more of a stroke than a blow, but the man staggered back as if I had pushed my whole weight against him. The last thing I saw was the look of astonishment on his face, and then I was off, running as fast as I could, afraid that he might come after me. I was too scared to look back, I just ran along the promenade, with the houses swinging around me like giant see-saws, and the sea on the left gaping at me like the jaws of a giant shark. I couldn't remember how I made my way back to the hotel; the next thing I became aware of was Mother leaning over me as I woke up in bed.

"Adam," she was saying, "what happened?"

"We must leave, Mother," I said. "We must leave this place at once."

"Don't be silly," she said and withdrew.

15

The next day we were already closer to our ruin, which I felt, was inevitable. It wasn't clear who struck the deal with the boatman: whether Mother, who fell for his spiel about the uninhabited island, or Father, who early in the morning brought the man to the hotel's dining room and treated him to a sumptuous breakfast. They chatted like old friends, exchanging jokes and fishing tales. In the end they ordered brandy and clinked their glasses as if drinking to a secret agreement.

During the journey on a puttering old fishing boat it became clear that Mother and Father had known the man from their previous holidays, from the days before I was born or was too small to remember. Talking to them, and with a rudder in his blistered hand, he looked almost human, much more so than during our meeting on the pier. Perhaps he was quite normal, after all, and the problem was once again my "hypertrophy of the senses".

"Don't you remember Simon?" Mother asked me with a touch of reproach.

"No, I don't. Can we go back now, please?"

"What's the matter with you? You've been acting strangely ever since we arrived. Is it those dreams again?" she turned to Father.

Father shrugged and looked at the island which suddenly emerged from the slight mist ahead. It was bare and rocky, just as Simon the boatman had described it. It lay before us like the exposed back of a large underwater animal, waiting quietly for unsuspecting holidaymakers to land on its surface. It was half past eleven when we pulled into a little cove on the southern end of the island. As soon as we disembarked, the boatman announced that he would carry on to the next little island, where he had to pick up a load of bricks; he would collect us on the way back some time in the afternoon.

Then it happened. Father suddenly waded into the sea and scrambled back into the boat. He said he would accompany Simon to the next island, where he would need help with the loading of bricks. As for Mother and me, we should be all right, what with the sun and the sea, and the whole island to explore.

"Don't you dare," Mother shouted. But it was too late; the boatman had started the motor and the boat pulled away from the shore as if pushed by an invisible force. Within minutes it was out in the open sea, bouncing on the waves and drawing away, with Father waving good-bye.

"He'll live to regret this," was all Mother could say.

For the first hour we swam in the clear waters of the bay. Then, stretched out on the pebbly beach, we allowed our bodies to be cooled by a gentle breeze and warmed by the weak sunshine. Mother fell asleep and started to snore. At first everything seemed normal, without any signs that something unusual may be afoot. Then, gradually, nature began to draw closer, silently, like a stalking animal, and I could feel the weight in the pit of my stomach growing heavier.

It started as I began to listen to the sounds of the sea. The waves would crash against the shore, fold in on themselves and retreat, but leave just enough water to come rushing up the beach to my feet, touch my heels with tentacles of cold and then slowly recede, rolling a few pebbles along into the depths, where it cowered until the next wave threw it back on the shore, spitting out the pebbles like undigested seeds. As it receded again, it dislodged others and rolled them to the edge of the beach, to the shallows, and some even further, swallowing them forever.

The thrusts of the sea varied, water did not reach my feet every time, occasionally it only dragged pebbles along, and now and then it would sink into itself, pausing as if the sea were taking a deep breath. But such intervals were not silent, they were filled with the sounds of the sea crashing against the rocks far away, for the waves were attacking the rocky shore in staggered forays, assaulting here and withdrawing there, causing a dissonance of thunderous splashes, sloshes, sprays and sprinkles which increasingly filled me with an awareness of the presence of evil, of something getting ready to harm either me or Mother, or both of us.

I looked at Mother. She was resting on her towel not far away, lying on her stomach in a yellow swimsuit, with her head in the crook of her arm and with her loose blond hair covering most of her shoulders, with the skin on the back of her legs the same hue of blue as the sea water before it produced white sprinkle and folded in on itself. Blue cold was creeping up her legs and slowly devouring her body. Eventually, her heart would freeze. And then she would stop worrying about me, berating me, sneaking after me, examining my bed sheets, checking my reading matter, double-checking my homework, barging into the bathroom while I was showering ... Then, yes, then it would only be Father, Eve and me. United in my dreams. Living happily ever after...

I turned away from the sea. Behind us was a gently rising hill, covered in boulders and pale rugged rocks, with patches of shrivelled grass here and there. On my right the hill continued into a long promontory, which jutted out into the sea, cradling the little cove like a protective arm. How big was the island? That I didn't know; on our way to the cove we had seen no more than its western side. I began to walk towards the top of the hill. I wanted to see what lay on the other side. I walked barefoot, stepping carefully to avoid getting cut on the sharp rocky surface. The sounds of the sea gradually weakened and became distant, almost inaudible. As I turned around I could barely see Mother's body in the cove below; it was tiny, insignificant, like the body of an unknown bather.

When I finally reached the top of the hill I could see at once that the island was much bigger than I had expected. An undulating surface of white-grey rocks and boulders, interspersed with rare tufts of grass, stretched out before me as far as the eye could see. Only far away was it possible to make out the vague shape of the mountain which towered above the little town we had come from. The distance was such that it would probably take me the best part of the day to walk to the other side of the island. I looked around to find the neighbouring island to which Father had gone with the boatman to help him load bricks. I looked in all directions but all I could se was the mainland on one side and open sea on the other. There was no neighbouring island.

I ran as fast as I could back down the slope, jumping from rock to rock, from boulder to boulder, caring little for grazes and cuts which my feet suffered on the way.

"Mother," I shouted when I reached the cove, "we've been left on the island!"

"What?" she mumbled, emerging from her stupor.

Suddenly everything had fallen into place! The way the boatman laughed before disappearing behind the promontory. That scornful look on his face during the journey to the island. The strange behaviour of the staff at the hotel. The heaviness, the sly persistence of the sea. We were superfluous, we had to be got rid of, and the boatman had been selected to take us to the bare island, and leave us there. Father must have realised this; why else would he have scrambled back into the boat at the last moment, if not to prevent the boatman from carrying out his evil deed, and to force him to return? By doing so he must have hastened his own end, for as soon as they were out in the open sea, the boatman must have pushed him overboard, after first hitting him on the head with an oar.

"Mother," I cried, "we're going to die!"

"Are you dreaming again?" she snapped. "They'll be here any minute, they must have got delayed by a bottle; you know what men are like."

"Mother, look at the sun. The night will be here in no time at all."

She rummaged in her carrier bag, pulled out her silver watch and stuck it under my nose. "Four o'clock. Why don't you go for a swim?"

"Mother," I whined, "we came at eleven."

"Or a walk," she said, stretching out on her towel.

I ran up the incline again, this time not to the top of the hill, but alongside it towards the promontory jutting into the sea, and over it to the other side, where I could see another little cove, and behind it a second, similar promontory, slightly lower than the first, and behind it a third, higher again, and behind that one, barely visible and almost the colour of the sky, a fourth and fifth, and behind those perhaps another, too distant to be seen in the haze. The island was very jagged, with a number of little coves and pebbly beaches, and suddenly I was filled with the hope that there might be other belated tourists in some of the coves, brought by other fishermen.

This gave me new strength and I hurried on, along the steep rocky incline, to get to the top of the second promontory, from where I might see people in the cove behind it. My feet were already badly cut and I was leaving a trail of blood drops on the rocks. Strangely, I did not feel any pain. A dry wind began to push in from the sea, spreading in random waves, most of which missed me by a yard or two, but those that hit me were so powerful that they nearly pushed me over.

When I reached the top of the promontory, I could see no one in the cove behind it. My disappointment was not too great; for some reason I was convinced that if there were signs of life on the island, I would find them only in the fourth or fifth cove. Although tired, I hurried on, this time toward the top of the hill again, suddenly hoping that from a higher vantage point I would see two or three coves at the same time. But when I reached the top my eyes beheld something I would not have expected to see even in a dream: a vast rocky plain spreading all the way to the horizon and beyond it, into an endless, invisible space. It was darkened in places by patches of withered grass. I turned around. The cove had vanished, and so had the sea; as if I were no longer on an island at all. The rocky surface was neither white nor grey, but vaguely bluish, like the colour of the sky.

Strewn around as far as I could see were sharp stones of various sizes. Barely perceptible waves of warm air travelled across the plane. The warmth wasn't caused by the sun; it reminded me of the heat waves produced by a powerful radiator fan. The wind was blowing into my face regardless of where I turned, as if the streams of air were coming from all directions at once, with their paths intersecting at the point I happened to be at any one time. I knew that my physics teacher would dismiss the idea as ludicrous, but that was the only explanation that made any sense.

Time did not seem to pass in this unfamiliar land, or, if it did, there wasn't the slightest sign that would confirm this. The land and the sky did not change their appearance; everything seemed to be standing still. I could feel neither thirst nor hunger, neither fear nor elation; definite proof that my body was no longer subject to natural laws. I felt like lying down and waiting for something to happen. In the end, however, it seemed better to walk, anywhere. Maybe far away, in the invisible distance, things were different, maybe I would at least meet animals, if not people, or angels, if this were the afterworld.

I closed my eyes and swivelled around. I walked in the direction I was facing as I opened my eyes. After five minutes of walking I got the strange feeling that I wasn't moving at all, for I seemed to be leaving nothing behind. The rocky surface under my feet seemed to be going past me, or coming toward me, and yet, in spite of the very long steps I was taking, I seemed to stay in the same place. I carried on anyway; in the end it made no difference whether I walked or stood still, especially as I did not feel any tiredness, not even after walking what seemed like ten miles.

Suddenly I noticed, lying among the stalks of withered grass, a large bone, smooth and shiny, definitely a human bone, a tibia. The world was no longer empty; I had found a trace of a living being: once, however long ago, the rocky plain had been visited by humans. Perhaps only one, who had wandered onto it by mistake, like myself, and couldn't find a way out. I picked up the bone and was surprised to discover that it was much heavier than I had expected. I decided to take it with me; if I were attacked I could use it as a bludgeon. Carrying a large human bone on my shoulder I felt safer, almost warm at heart.

A few minutes later, I came upon what at first looked like a large patch of grass, but upon closer inspection turned out to be a small pond, filled with very dark water which was ruffled by the criss-crossing winds in the most unusual pattern of tiny wavelets. Sitting in the middle of it on a large oak leaf was a creature with the head of a frog and the body of a three-year old baby, beautiful, pink, with tiny legs crossed lotus fashion, like a small Buddha. Lying in its plump, tiny arms was an open book.

I stepped to the edge of the water and leaned forward to decipher the words on the title page. I could just make out *My Father's Dreams*, but the author's name was tucked away in the top corner. The book must have been very interesting, for the creature was so engrossed in it that it remained completely unaware of my presence. I wondered whether to tiptoe past it or try to engage it in conversation; this was after all the first living being I had encountered in this empty world. It seemed unlikely that it would attack me; and if it did, I could easily defend myself with the large bone. Curiosity prevailed; I raised the tibia and brought it down on the water to cause a loud splash.

But there was no splash; the bone hit the ground, as if the water was not real at all, but painted on the stony surface. This was confirmed by the sound of the blow, which forced the creature to raise its eyes above the book and look at me. It did so visibly frightened, but also with a strange, muted joy, as if it had recognized me from some previous meeting. Then its eyes grew dark once again, expressing only deep sadness and detachment. The creature returned to reading the book. I brought the bone down once more, but again there was only a thud instead of a splash; the water was definitely an illusion. I stepped on it; my foot did not sink.

I stepped on it with both feet and started to jump up and down. Nothing. I walked to the middle of the pond and poked with the bone at the creature's face. The bone scraped against stone. The creature looked at me again, this time from very close and almost from under my feet. The bone was resting on its head without touching it; as though the scene were projected on the ground from above.

I crossed the pond to the other side and turned around. The creature was not turning its back to me, as I had expected, but was facing me as before, still reading the same book and paying no attention to me at all. I circled the pond. No matter where I stopped, the creature remained in the same position, always facing me, always showing me only the cover of the book. All my attempts to get behind it and peek over its shoulder to see what the book was about ended in failure. But if the whole scene was projected from above, why did the creature notice me, follow my moves, and react independently from the projection? There was something here that was beyond my powers to understand.

But the creature suddenly ceased to look strange and unfamiliar; it began to remind me of my little brother Abortus. Not so much the one in the glass jar; more the one I dreamed about while writing a composition at school. I lay down beside the pond and closed my eyes. I began to suspect that all this was a dream. I was hoping that if I managed to fall asleep I might start dreaming about the real world again, or at least about the world which others thought to be real. The world of Father, Mother, and Eve. And of Abortus in the glass jar, not the projected one, but my real brother.

16

The first thing I felt was the sea water as it nibbled coldly at my feet and retreated with the sound of rolling pebbles. Next there was a pause, during which I could hear the distant sound of the sea hurling its waves against the rocks. As I opened my eyes I saw Mother sitting on her towel only two yards away, nervously smoking. She was depositing ashes in a paper container she had made from the remains of a magazine. It was spilling over with cigarette butts; she must have finished an entire packet. But even here, in the middle of nowhere, condemned to a slow death, she remained staunchly loyal to her need for order and tidiness.

The sun had set and the sea had grown sombre and threatening. The rocky surface of the island was fast disappearing in the jaws of the night which was creeping across the swaying waters.

"Were you dreaming?" Mother asked. As she looked at me I thought I saw traces of tears on her face, but they must have been marks caused by the sun.

I shrugged and looked at the heaving darkness beyond the cove.

"I know you were," she said. "You trembled and mumbled strange words in your sleep." She drew on the end of her cigarette once more and carefully placed the butt on top of the others.

"Are you hungry?" she asked.

She reached in her carrier bag and pulled out the bun she had refused to leave behind during breakfast. She split it in half and reached out to give me my share. Then we sat chewing our halves of the stale bun without saying a word.

Darkness was slowly thickening. Mother put her right hand on top of her head and slowly smoothed her hair until she reached the nape of the neck, where she let her hand rest for a while. And suddenly something happened. I don't know if it was her gesture, which was nothing unusual, for it was almost a habit for her to stroke her hair like that, but something made me realise with a shock that Mother existed. That she had a life of her own. That she was more than a mere shape in my thoughts. That she was not my invention, or the annoying shadow she had so often seemed, or the cook and cleaner that could always be disregarded as just being there by the laws of nature. Whichever way I had perceived her, she had never been as real as Father.

Now she had suddenly turned into a person whose presence was not defined by the wishes and needs of Father and me. A person who had her own desires, plans, anxieties, maybe connected with Father and me, but independent of us. Those twists of blond hair I would sometimes find in the toilet bowl were not merely something that I could aim my piss at; they were combed-out bits of hair from the head which at night rested next to Father's and often, at night as well as in daytime, pondered our common future, Father's disinterest, my lack of interest in school, my introversion, my dreams which bothered her most, and, perhaps above all, the good name of our family.

I looked at her just as she swallowed the last piece of the bun and clapped her hands to get rid of the crumbs. For the first time in my life I realised that Mother was actually rather beautiful and still young; with smooth skin which was perhaps only around her eyes showing traces of a life-long dependence on tranquilisers and nicotine. Every other part of her body was still firm and taut, even her thighs; a well-preserved body of a tall, slim, forty-year old woman. For the first time in my life I felt something warm in my heart as I looked at her. It occurred to me that now, perhaps, I could ask her why we never mentioned my unborn little brother Abortus. Now, I felt, she would not brush me off by saying that she had no idea what I was talking about.

But she spoke a fraction of a second before I opened my mouth.

"Well," she said, "they must have drunk each other under the table. We're unlikely to see them before first light. I know you don't like it if I say anything bad about Father, but I'll never forgive him for leaving us here to spend a cold night in the open."

"It's not Father's fault," I shouted, and the closeness I felt a moment earlier evaporated like passing mist. "It's the boatman, who pushed Father off the boat and let him drown in the sea! We're going to die on this island!"

"Don't be stupid," she berated me in her usual tone of voice. "We've known Simon for years. The only one who might be tempted to get rid of us is your Father. And I wouldn't put it past him that that's what he has decided to do."

She paused for a moment. Then her voice surged as if lifted by an incoming wave.

"You don't realise what a bother we are to him, Adam. He won't talk to me because he thinks I'm stupid, a servant to take care of him that he could just as well hire. And as for you, he can't stand you because of those dreams of yours he can't cure. Simon is okay, it's your Father who can't be trusted."

"Shut up, Mother," I said and started to cry. "Don't talk like that about Father. He is the best father anyone could have."

"And I'm the worst Mother, I suppose?" she retorted.

"Maybe," I heard myself saying.

She said nothing, she just started to cry.

As soon as she started I stopped; I didn't want to cry with her. I realised that in spite of the earlier moment of closeness I really hated my Mother, and would have forgiven Father for leaving her on the island to die. Of course he would never have left me on the island, so Mother's idea was really an indication of the hatred she felt for Father, because of which my hatred of her seemed all the more justified. As we were swallowed by the black night, damp and cold with sporadic bursts of sea spray, I concluded that it was in fact Mother's fault we had been left on the island, for she was the one who had insisted on coming. I knew that the boatman was evil the moment I saw him.

When the moon appeared from behind the hill, reminding me of the twisted face of a starving baby, I realised that, without Mother and her interference, and without my constant fear that she might discover my diary, Father, Eve and I could be happy in my dreams for a long time to come. It was Mother who was spoiling the happiness of all three of us. And the only reason she got rid of Abortus before he could be born as a normal baby must have been her decision that I didn't deserve a brother.

The night was quite chilly, but we didn't dress. We sat on our towels and stared at the heaving darkness before us. Then we lay on our backs, staring at the sky which resembled a huge star-cobbled vault. Then we lay with our backs against each other, then Mother lay on her stomach while I sat up, then she sat and I lay on my stomach, then she walked off into darkness but soon returned, and then gradually things became vague and misty, and I was enveloped by a curious veil of uncertainty in which again I wasn't quite sure what was a dream and what reality.

In the middle of the night we became thirsty. The plastic bottle of water which Mother had brought along more by accident than design lay between us like a growing sign of the coming conflict. We both knew we could share the water, and we both knew we should share it. But we made a decision to fight for it. Half the water could mean three additional days of life. It was I who managed to wrestle the bottle from Mother's hands and keep it. I drank half the water at once. I pressed the bottle with the other half to my chest with both hands, watching Mother's every move like a hawk.

We both knew we would die on the island. No one would pick us up, and it was much too far to swim to the mainland. While thinking about how to spend the remaining time, our fear and hatred of each other slowly melted away and we became ashamed of our feelings. We crawled toward each other and began to comfort and caress each other like two mortally wounded animals. I could suddenly feel that Mother's cheeks were soft, that her lips were hot, that her skin smelled like Eve's.

While she held me tightly and sobbed, "Adam, Adam," I kept pressing the mouth of the bottle to her lips, begging her to drink. "Drink, Mother, drink." She did, and I felt happy. She didn't drink all the water, she left some for me. Again I felt happy. Those bright moments of kindness in the gathering darkness made our fear of the inevitable almost bearable. We did not want to die, but there were no selfish thoughts in our fight for life any more; we just wanted to give, to sacrifice for each other all we had, to turn ourselves into parting presents for one another.

Then, unexpectedly, hatred flooded back like a huge tidal wave. We jumped on each other like two ravenous beasts, with mouths stuck together as if trying to suck the last drops of moisture from the already dry lips, with fingers intertwined and twisted as in a violent wrestling match, with body thrusting at body in a murderous passion, and with teeth and nails sunk deep in the skin everywhere our hands could find support. In spite of the cold we became hot and sweaty, licking drops of perspiration off each other's body for thirst. And as we started to die both at once, as we felt the cramp spreading from head to toe, the pain of leaving was not half as horrible as I had expected, it was sweet, sweeter than anything I had ever encountered. When, in a tight embrace and with nails still dug in each other's skin, we started to sink into darkness, I felt a great surge of relief and forgiveness for the sins and mistakes of life, and a promise of peace, the warm peace of total darkness.

But eventually the darkness dissipated and we were nudged awake by the bright morning sun. Far from any heaven, our immediate surroundings were precisely what we had hoped to escape: a lifeless rocky island, and a turbulent sea crashing against the shore. But the night had brought something new: swaying in the quieter waters of the cove was a small sailing boat. Standing on board was a bearded sea captain in dark-blue uniform, with gold stripes that were clearly visible in the sun. In his left hand he held a cigar, in the right one a half raised telescope.

"Grandpa Dominic!" I shouted.

He heard me and waved. Then, as if satisfied, he slowly stroked his long beard, drew on the cigar and puffed the smoke into the fresh morning air.

On our way back to the mainland he explained what had brought him. After hearing that we had unexpectedly left for a holiday at sea he enquired at the surgery where we had gone. Overcome by a great yearning to smell the sea wind and hear the crashing of waves he had followed us down by train. At the hotel he had managed to unearth what appeared to be a big secret: that Simon the fisherman had taken us to an uninhabited island. He had decided to wait for us, but when my Father and Simon returned alone he wanted to know what had become of Mother and me. Father and Simon had told him that we had decided to spend the night in a little fishing village on an island from where Simon regularly transported bricks. But a little later, after a brief private discussion, they admitted that they had left us on an uninhabited island all day and night because they wanted to frighten us, as a joke, of course, so that I would have something to boast about when I went back to school.

In the end they had even agreed with Grandpa Dominic's suggestion that the joke was a little thin, and promised to fetch us immediately. But he, an old sailor, had hired a boat and beaten them to it.

"I am used to rescuing castaways," he laughed.

I embraced him and thanked him profusely.

"You'll be all right," he said, running his coarse hand over my hair.

As I looked up at his eyes, kind and soft as always, I could see a hint of evasion in his look: as if he had told us only half of what he knew.

17

Coming home was a shock. Although things looked familiar, they appeared unfriendly and strange, as if belonging in someone else's life, or in a time from which I had been severed, the way a severed head is divorced from the body. For some days even Abortus appeared strangely distant. No matter how hard I tried to force myself, I could not tell him about all the things that happened. I was unsure what had really happened, and what was merely a dream. I decided not to write anything in my diary until the confusion cleared.

To be fair to myself, I had almost no opportunity to get at my diary. Since returning from holidays, Father took to spending his afternoons and sometimes evenings as well with his bonsai experiments in the basement. At home, where he was now coming only to eat, sleep and infect the house with malevolence, as Mother would occasionally reproach him, things had also become very different. We all kept to ourselves, the house was filled with ominous silence, and we almost deliberately avoided each other. When, more by accident than design, we found ourselves together at the dining table, Father would prop up a book in front of his plate and peer into it like a schoolboy facing an exam the following day. I noticed that often he peered at one page much longer than it would have taken him to read it at a leisurely speed.

But the strangest of all was Mother's reticence, so unlike her that I often wondered what could have caused it. Her habitual nagging and scolding had become a memory; even the disorder I left behind in the bathroom every morning no longer moved her to tell me off. Whenever our eyes accidentally met, she would avert hers as if suddenly noticing something that demanded her instant attention.

At school no one believed that I had been ill. In a small village like ours it would have been impossible to hide the fact that we had gone on holiday. But no one had the courage to say anything. Everybody knew that sooner or later they would have to knock at the door of Father's surgery; either themselves or their children, parents, aunts, uncles or distant cousins. No one was in a hurry to upset the only doctor for miles around. Only my language teacher asked me, as if in passing, when I would write a composition about my latest dream: would that by any chance be a dream about seasickness?

Grandpa Dominic had refused to come back with us; he said he wanted to stay a few days at the sea, now that he was there, and besides, he had a return train ticket anyway. Every day while returning from school I would take a longer route to walk past his house, to see if he had come back. After five days I started to worry that something had happened to him, or that he had decided to make one more sea voyage, his last. Then, two days later, as I walked up the road towards the house, I noticed that the main door was wide open. I ran the rest of the way and stormed into the house, calling out at the top of my voice, "Grandpa Dominic, Grandpa Dominic!"

Silence greeted my words. The air in the house was less stuffy than during my previous visits; a window must have been opened somewhere at the opposite end, with the draught filling the rooms with the fresh smell of an October afternoon. Perhaps, I thought, he had fallen asleep in the big chair in the living room. But the chair was empty. In the beam of sunlight entering through the gap in the drawn curtains I noticed that three of the African gods were missing.

Perhaps there were burglars in the house, looting Grandpa Dominic's valuables! I followed the stream of fresh air to its source and discovered that it was coming in through the bathroom window which was wide open. The door was ajar. As I tried to push it open I felt resistance; something heavy on the other side refused to yield. I hurled all my weight against it, to no avail. In the end I managed to push the door open just wide enough for my head to squeeze through the gap.

At first I refused to believe my eyes. Lying on the wet floor of the bathroom was Eve, her head resting on the edge of the bathtub, her legs outstretched and pushing against the door. She was wearing a short blue-grey frock which had curled up under her into a wet mound of material impregnated with something dark. I realised that the wetness on the floor was not water; it was a large thin patch of diluted blood. Then I saw blood seeping from a severed vein on the wrist of Eve's left arm, which lay, together with the right one, in her lap as if neither belonged to her. Her eyes were closed, and her body was shivering.

"Eve!" I yelled.

She raised her eyelids and watched me through the narrow gaps as if trying to remember who I was. The pallor of her sunken cheeks gave her look a piercing edge.

"It's you," she finally breathed. "Come, join me on my way to a beautiful dream. Are you afraid?"

She closed her eyes again and the puddle on the floor was slowly spreading. I knew what had to be done; I had seen such scenes in Father's surgery often enough. I ran to the kitchen and grabbed the nearest dish cloth. It was filthy and had a stale, sour smell, but there was no time to look for another. I pushed my head through the gap into the bathroom and shouted:

"Raise your legs, Eve! Pull them up, bend your knees!"

She half opened her eyes but immediately closed them again; she failed to understand what I wanted. I hurled myself against the door and managed to push it open another ten inches, but Eve's legs immediately straightened out again and pushed the door back. I tried again and this time wedged my body into the widened gap. I managed to squeeze through. I knelt down in the puddle of blood and tightly bandaged her wrist with a dishcloth.

"Adam," she breathed and half raised her eyelids. "Make sure you don't die a virgin. Sinning is sweet."

I pushed my hands under her arms and tried to lift her, but she was too heavy, her body limp. I stepped into the bathtub, from which the dripping tap had already washed away most of the blood, and pushed my hands under her arms from behind. This didn't work either, I simply wasn't strong enough.

"Adam," I heard her say, "leave me, I'm okay, I feel fine."

I climbed out of the bathtub, grabbed her legs and pushed them up by bending them at the knees, just enough to open the door.

"Wait here," I told her, as if this were at all necessary. "Don't move."

I knew there was no phone in the house, so I decided to run to the health centre and ask Father to jump in the car and get straight back to save Eve while there was still time. But just as I came out of the house I saw a tractor with a trailer bouncing past on the rough road, with the driver sitting on the high seat and staring ahead as if the rest of the world did not exist. I ran alongside the huge wheel, shouting and waving my arms until the man noticed me. Even then it took more than a minute before he decided to believe my story, and another minute for him to reverse the vehicle back to the house.

We brought Eve, who in the meantime had become unconscious, out of the house and lifted her onto the empty trailer. I climbed in with her and held her head in my lap, so that during the drive down the rough road it wouldn't roll around. I felt her pulse; it was weak, but the heart was still beating.

"Faster!" I yelled at the farmer. "Faster!"

"Next time stop a Mercedes," was his reply. After that he remained stubbornly silent until we reached the health centre. I asked him to sound the horn.

Nurse Mary was the first who came running out. She was followed by Father, and all three of us lifted Eve from the trailer and carried her up the stairs into the surgery. I was more in the way than of any help, so I just ran along, every now and then pushing away a stray lock of hair that kept sliding over Eve's eyes. As soon as Father and Nurse Mary brought her into the surgery and placed her on the examining table, she opened her eyes and looked straight at me.

"Adam," she said, "why didn't you let me go? I wanted to go to the place where everybody is loved by at least one other person."

But I love you, Eve, I wanted to shout, I will always love you, I am that other person, the only person who really loves you. But I had to keep the words inside me, I couldn't let them come out in front of Nurse Mary and Father. Especially Father, who was already measuring Eve's blood pressure.

"Adam," he said without looking at me, "out."

"But Father ..." I tried to object.

"Nurse," he snapped, "get him out of the surgery."

Nurse Mary placed her hands on my shoulders, turned me around, and pushed me towards the door and out into the waiting room. She slammed the door behind me with such force that the waiting patients looked at me as if it was my fault that Eve had decided to cut her wrist. Maybe it is, I thought. Maybe I don't love her enough.

I ran out into the courtyard and round the corner. I climbed the fire-escape stairs to the wooden hatch and climbed into the loft. I crawled as far as the chimney and peered through the gap in the ceiling into the surgery. The examining table was right below. The blood-soaked dish cloth from Grandpa Dominic's kitchen lay on the floor. Nurse Mary was dressing Eve's wrist with disinfected surgical gauze. Father was sitting at Nurse Mary's table, leaning on it with his elbow and supporting his head with his hand. He looked as if the sudden event had exhausted him.

When Nurse Mary finished and began to tidy up, Father said, "Nurse, go to the dispensary and bring some iron tablets. And tranquilisers, I recommend diazepam."

Nurse Mary tried to explain that she would do that as soon as she tidied up, but Father cut her short, "Now, Nurse, this very moment."

Nurse Mary dropped everything she held in her hands on the floor and demonstratively walked out of the room. Father, Eve and I were alone now. For a while there was silence.

Then Father asked, "Why did you do it?"

Eve did not move. The bandaged arm lay next to her limp and lifeless, as if she had disowned it. In her eyes, too, there was hardly any life; she was looking straight up, not at the gap, through which I was peering into the surgery, but past it through the ceiling, through the roof, through the sky into eternity which we had not allowed her to enter. How sincerely she wanted to enter it I could not tell. Even less clear was what could have happened to her to make eternity tempting. This wasn't clear to Father, either, for after a pause he repeated his question.

He got up, approached the examining table and looked at Eve with an expression of deep concern, almost fear.

As soon as Father came close enough for Eve to touch him I felt a familiar thud in my head. I knew that I had crossed the boundary from the waking state into a dream. The surgery became misty and unfamiliar, as though it had been moved from the health centre to some other building. I expected the dream to continue in the usual way, with Father slowly sliding his fingers under Eve's skirt, or with her reaching out and unzipping his fly. But Father merely stood and watched her, while Eve turned her head away as if unwilling to face him.

"Why?" Father repeated less harshly, in a tone which was not far from despair. "And why are you here? Why aren't you at home, with your parents, where you should be?"

"You know why I'm here," she turned her face towards him. "Because of you."

"Certainly not because of me," Father said. He turned away and made a few steps around the surgery. "You're here because of what you need, but that I can't give you any more."

"Why not?" demanded Eve in a weak voice. "Why can't you give me what you've been giving me for the last three months? You don't like me any more. That's why. No one likes me, not my parents, not you, not the friends I used to have. I'm alone. Where can I go? You must give me what I need, I have been good to you, I will continue to be good."

Father, who had been staring out of the window, abruptly turned and half shouted, half hissed, "Stop it!"

He went to the door and turned the key in the lock.

"Stop," he continued more quietly, "playing on these worn-out sentimental strings, because I'm not going to fall for it any more. Do you realise what you've turned me into? And my family? You've turned me into a monster that shivers at the thought of what he could've done if it wasn't for your grandfather. A monster that lives in daily dread of being found out, and will do anything to prevent that. Does that make you happy? I'm responsible for five hundred patients, do you realise what that means?"

"That means you're also responsible for me," Eve replied, "because I'm one of your patients. You agreed to treat me; you can't just throw me out when it suits you. Or stuff me into one of those jars in the basement. Is that what you'd like to do?"

For a moment Father disappeared from my area of vision and returned with a syringe in his right hand.

"You could've bled to death, do you realise that?"

He looked for a vein in the crook of her arm and slowly injected the clear liquid into her bloodstream.

"This is the last time," he said. "I can't go on. I'll take you back to your grandfather's house. Pull yourself together, go back to your parents, go back to school, go and kick your habit somewhere they take care of people like you. If you carry on like this, you'll die."

"We're all going to die," she said. "You as well. Death is the only beautiful thing in the world. Do you want your reward now or later, back at the house?"

"Keep your reward," Father said and removed his white coat. "Shall we go?"

"I wonder," said Eve, carefully placing her legs on the floor, "how long you'll be able to do without."

"I'll castrate myself, if that's the only way," Father said and pushed her toward the door.

As soon as they left the surgery I expected my dream to end. But nothing happened, I could feel no movement or switchover inside my head. Was it a dream? Or was it all real? I was no longer sure. In the end I decided that it was a dream, all I had to do was catch up with it. Losing no time, I scrambled out through the hatch, tumbled down the fire-escape stairs and ran in a straight line across the fields and orchards toward Grandpa Dominic's house. I was almost sure now that the dream would continue, and I wanted to be there in time not to miss any of it.

At one of the farms I passed I was nearly frightened to death by a huge growling dog that came bearing down on me with his teeth showing. Just before reaching me he was held back by the chain. His growling and barking followed me until I reached the edge of Grandpa Dominic's orchard. At that moment I realised that I was too late; Father's car had just turned onto the road and sped back to the village.

The main door was closed but not locked. My first destination was the bathroom; I was afraid that I would find Eve on the floor as before, in an even bigger puddle of blood. But the bathroom was empty; the spots on the tiles had already dried. I ran up the stairs to the first floor and to the end of the corridor. The door to Eve's room was open.

I found her lying on the bed with eyes closed. Her arms were stretched out by her side. She looked rigid, like a drowned person who had just been pulled out of water and laid out on the grass. In the corner of the room I noticed a little knapsack with which she must have arrived from the city. I knelt down beside the bed and watched her. I suppressed the sudden urge to touch her, but in the end I couldn't resist it; I gently placed my forefinger on her knee and slowly moved it up towards the hem of her dress. She winced, opened her eyes and looked straight at me.

"My knight in shining armour," she said with relief, barely audible. "The hero who defeated the dragon of eternal darkness and brought me back to the world of beauty and meaning."

Suddenly she sat up and drew me toward her. She put her arms round my neck and pressed her pale cheek against mine. She was all cold and limp. But her breath, which I felt in my ear, was hot and sweet.

"Adam," she breathed, "you'll have to help me, you will, won't you?"

I shrugged; I hadn't the slightest idea what she meant.

"You must, you simply must do something for me," she said.

"I can, in a dream," I said. "In a dream everything's possible and allowed. It's impossible to do anything wrong in a dream."

She pushed me away and looked at me sternly as if I had said something she disagreed with or could not understand. Then she nodded, as if concluding that my words were of no consequence after all.

"Adam, you'll have to bring me, and keep bringing me those things I used to get from your Father. Really, Adam, you'll have to. Because your father won't give them to me any more. He keeps them in little ampoules somewhere in his surgery. You will find them, won't you?"

I said that this would be quite impossible, since I did not have a key to the surgery.

"Adam," she pulled me back to herself, almost embracing me, "you'll find a way, I'm sure you will, promise you will. And then we shall dream together. Just you and me. And what I used to do with your Father, I will in future do only with you. Would you like that?"

I shrugged.

"Of course you would. And then you could write the dream down in your diary. Every little detail. Promise?"

I nodded.

She slid off the bed, stood up and looked out of the window.

"But not here," she said. "We couldn't dream here. The house is closely guarded by the African gods."

I told her that three were missing; someone must have broken in and stolen them.

"Fat chance," she said. "Grandpa has put them out, so they would scare off young men trying to sneak into the house and make off with my virginity. One is standing near the pond, the other near the front entrance, and the third at the bottom of the orchard. Haven't you seen them?"

"No", I said, "I haven't." I must have been too much in a hurry every time I came rushing into the house.

"Grandpa thinks that I'm pure, the kind of ideal granddaughter he'd like to have. Well, sorry, grandpa. Your granddaughter just isn't that kind of girl. You're old; you've lost touch with reality."

I wanted to say that, on the contrary, it was Grandpa Dominic who seemed to be the most in touch with reality, but she went on.

"That's the reason I prefer to be here. At home I can't even breathe. My parents know me too well. Although they don't really care. Do you think they'd be upset if I died today? Not in the least. They'd get some peace at last. They wouldn't have to be ashamed of my mega success at school. No, it's much nicer here. Much, much nicer. Also because of you," she put her hand on top of my head, stopping short of stroking my hair.

The touch of her hand was brief and, at least it seemed to me, slightly forced. But it filled me with soft, pleasant warmth.

"Do you know where we're going to dream?" she suddenly remembered. "On the wall by the stream. Where we almost started, and would've started, if your father hadn't come between us. The dream could easily have been ours alone. It may be partly my fault that it wasn't. But it's too late now. We can only find a way back by starting again. It'll be just as nice as it would've been if none of this ever happened."

Once again she reached out to stroke me, and once again she withdrew her hand; as if afraid that she was promising too much too early.

"Three ampoules," she said. "And a syringe. You mustn't forget the syringe."

Before I got the chance to explain how impossible this would be, she put her arm round my neck and began to suck at my lips with her mouth as if trying to suffocate me. The sensation was far from unpleasant. I wouldn't have minded if she never stopped. But she did.

She pushed me away and said:

"You don't know how to kiss. I'll have to teach you."

She collapsed back on the bed, ending up in the position in which I had found her.

"I'm so tired," she said. "I must have a sleep. Come tomorrow. And don't forget."

This was the last opportunity to pull out of the deal I never made, although she had got it into her head that I did. But as I searched for the right words I could see that they would be to no avail; she had already fallen asleep. I crouched by the bed for another ten minutes, watching her. She seemed very fragile, much more so than one would have thought by the sound of her voice.

At that moment it became clear to me that I had no choice; I would have to bring her the ampoules she wanted so much.

18

But how to get into the surgery? To steal Father's keys in the middle of the night seemed impossible; he was a light sleeper, and he kept the surgery keys on his bedside table. To lure him and Nurse Mary out of the surgery on some pretext was equally far-fetched; I would need at least a few minutes to find a syringe and the right ampoules. Besides, the glass cabinet in which he kept them was probably locked.

The only option remaining was to break in. To get through the door would be difficult; I would have to break it down, or break the lock, which would create a lot of noise. Besides, I would have to break down two doors, first the main one and then the surgery door; far too much for an inexperienced fourteen-year old burglar. That left the window.

Late at night, when I was fairly certain that both Mother and Father were asleep, I sneaked out of the house and ran barefoot and in pyjamas down to the village, hoping that no one would be about. In the shaking light of the torch – I had taken it from a cupboard in the hall – I managed to reach the health centre without stumbling or injuring my feet on the rough surface of the road. I soon discovered that the surgery window was much too high, and there was nothing I could grab hold of to climb up. What to do? Looking around I noticed a large metal container on wheels, used for depositing rubbish at the end of each working day. It was only half full, so it required little effort to wheel it under the window and climb onto it. From there it was easy to get onto the window sill.

But the window was closed on the inside, and the only way to get in was to break the glass. This could be dangerous, and I had nothing with which to do it; the torch did not seem the right tool. Again I was in a quandary. But not for long: I remembered reading about a burglary in one of the many books in Father's library, and did exactly what the burglar did in the story. I removed my pyjama top, wrapped it round my right fist and hit the pane so hard that it shattered. I removed the pyjama top, put it back on, reached inside to find the handle, and opened the window. Another few moments, and I was in the surgery.

In the beam of the torchlight I soon discovered what I was looking for: the big medicine chest with a glass door, secured with a padlock, as expected. It was not really glass but Perspex, impossible to break with a fist. I picked up a chair and smashed it against the front of the chest. To my dismay, it was the chair that broke, while the Perspex sustained no more than a graze. I looked around for a sturdier chair, and found one with metal legs. But as I swung the chair against the door the legs bounced off the Perspex as if made of rubber. What to do? I pointed my torchlight into every part of the surgery, but could find nothing that would serve the purpose. Sensing defeat I became angry and kicked against the chest with my bare foot. Miraculously, this move dislodged the padlock, which jumped off its hook and fell on the floor. Evidently it hadn't been pressed together, but merely placed on the hook in such a way as to create the impression that it was locked.

It wasn't difficult to find the ampoules containing Eve's medicine; all the other containers were labelled boxes. There were nine ampoules altogether, and I took them all. All I needed now was a syringe. As if by chance I remembered that earlier in the afternoon Father had thrown one into the rubbish bin after injecting Eve with the dose he described as the last one. Fortunately the cleaning lady had not emptied the bin. I rummaged among pungent blood-stained bandages, tissues and other unpleasant things until I found it, lying right at the bottom, undamaged. Now I had all I had come for.

The next morning I stayed in bed until I heard Father and Mother leave for work, Father first and Mother half an hour later. Then, my spirits higher than in many months, I made myself a sumptuous breakfast of bacon and eggs, and ate it with slow, deliberate attention; as if performing a sacred ritual. Feeling pleased with myself gave me a sense of composure and lightness, of floating in air. Finally I slung my bag over the shoulder and set off in the direction of school. Halfway up the hill I looked back and saw a police car in front of the health centre; the break-in had been reported, and the police were already checking the place for fingerprints. I felt secure; I could not imagine that anyone would suspect the doctor's son.

Just below the school I turned right into the wood, and walked through it, following the path along which Eve had taken me to Grandpa Dominic's house for the first time. I could still remember every detail of that walk, every smell, every slant of the sun rays, and I could see Eve's image dancing before me as clearly as if she were there. I walked on air, filled with anticipation to which I could not put a name. As I walked up the driveway towards the door I suddenly noticed the huge statue of one of the African gods. It was standing on the grass near the corner of the house, and it was the largest and most fearsome of the twelve tribal deities, a hermaphrodite with a jutting penis and large, pendulous breasts, with eyes that seemed to follow my every move me as I walked to the door.

"I'm a bearer of gifts," I explained as I walked up the stairs.

It was past nine o'clock, but Eve was still fast asleep, lying in the position in which I had left her. I did not want to wake her; I knelt down by the bed, rested my behind on the back of my shoes, and watched her. Watching Eve while she was asleep was a pleasure I could compare to nothing else. Overnight her cheeks had gained a barely noticeable rosy glow. She was wearing the same blue-grey frock, which had been pushed up as she was turning, exposing her left thigh all the way to the hip.

I could not take my eyes off that thigh. Remembering that it would soon become part of my reward, I reached in my bag and pulled out the syringe and one of the ampoules, placing both under the lamp on the bedside table. I had decided to give her an ampoule a day, no more, assuming that that was the dose Father would have prescribed. I had no idea what the liquid was, or what Father was treating her for, but he would hardly have given her something she did not need.

I had lost all sense of time. I looked out at the pale October sunshine, at the rusty colours of autumn which filled me with unfamiliar sadness. Something was saying good-bye, something was leaving me. As I looked at Eve's face and listened to her quiet breathing, I couldn't escape the feeling that she, too, was saying good-bye to me, and that our time had accelerated towards autumn before it got the chance to develop into spring. Perhaps it was already too late for the dream Eve had promised me.

I continued to watch her until she produced a deep sigh, shivered slightly and opened her eyes. For some time, searching for anything that would remind her of where she was, her eyes wandered around the room until they came to rest on my face.

"Still here?" she showed surprise, not quite sure that I was real.

I told her that a whole night had passed. And in that night many unusual events had taken place: the fruits of my daring escapade are on her bedside table. Slowly, she turned her head. When she saw the ampoule and the syringe, her body shot up as if a spring had suddenly been released inside it.

"No!" she shrieked, fully awake now. "You're a wonder! Come here, let me give you a hug." And she stretched her arms toward me in a move that was an order as much as a request.

I nearly sank in her embrace. She smelled of stale sweat, sour but also pleasantly sweet; she had obviously not washed for days. The softness of her cheek, which she pressed against mine, was heavenly beyond description.

"You'll be my hero," she whispered into my ear. "You'll supply me with medicine for my wounded soul. We'll never leave this place. The African gods will guard us."

Then she grabbed the syringe and the ampoule and got to work, trembling with excitement. But the fingers of her left hand had grown stiff because of the bandaged wrist, and would not obey her.

"Help me, Adam," she held out the ampoule and the syringe, "you should know, you're a doctor's son."

I was, and I did not want to let her down. I pushed the needle through the plastic seal and drew out half the liquid, putting the ampoule back on the bedside table. I reached for Eve's arm. First she offered me the left, the bandaged one, which bore the traces of all the earlier injections. Then she pulled it back and offered me the right one.

"Let this be a new beginning. Ours."

I found the vein and slowly pressed on the plunger until I was sure that all of the liquid had entered Eve's bloodstream. She emitted a deep sigh, closed her eyes and leaned her head back as far as it would go. Then she let it fall forward on to her chest, shaking it, so that her matted locks loosened and bobbed up and down. She took my hand, pulled it into her lap and looked closely into my eyes.

"And now the dream. This one will be the nicest you've ever had. I've decided so."

After that things became a little unclear, perhaps because of the feeling that the dream had started the moment Eve announced it, strengthened by the nimble gesture with which she pulled off her dress over her head. Then she did the same with the tiny slip she was wearing underneath, and finally with her panties, which gave her more trouble, because she had to wiggle out of them. But in the end she stretched out before me naked, as naked as I remembered her from my dreams, except that this time she hadn't undressed for Father.

"What are you waiting for?" she looked at me. "In dreams we are never dressed. In dreams we are free of shame. Innocent as God made us."

I began to undress. Not knowing what to do with my clothes, I dropped them on the floor. She kicked hers to the bottom of the bed. As I stretched out next to her, she placed her fingers round my penis and squeezed it.

"I'll never let go of it. I'll make it grow until it reaches the size of the one on the African god which is guarding the entrance."

But the god was not very good at guarding, for the next moment two men walked in through the open door: Grandpa Dominic, and someone who looked like Eve's father. Behind them, still in the corridor, I noticed the face of a policeman who failed to hide a lewd expression at the sight of our bodies. The first thing Eve's father fixed his eyes on was the half-empty ampoule and the syringe on the bedside table. His gaze was followed by that of Grandpa Dominic, and finally of the policeman, who in the meantime had entered the room.

Then all three of them looked at me. Embarrassed, I looked at the ceiling; not because of the ampoule and the syringe, which were, after all, part of Eve's medical treatment, but because of my exposed penis which was pointing into the air as if standing to attention. But then I remembered that this was only a dream, it wasn't real, so I relaxed and even managed to smile at the three astonished faces.

"Eve, put your clothes on," the man who looked like Eve's Father ordered in a dry voice. "We're leaving."

I remember that later that afternoon I wrote into my dream diary how terribly Eve shrieked and cried as they dragged her out of the room and downstairs and out of the house, in front of which a police car was parked next to a black Mercedes.

"Adam!" she shouted as she looked up at the window at the end of the corridor, to which I was desperately pressing my face. Before she was pushed into the back seat of the Mercedes, I only just caught her words, the very last I would hear:

"Whenever you think of me you must smile! That's an order!"

19

Because there wasn't a moment I didn't think of her, smiling became such a habit for me that in the end I became powerless to resist it no matter how hard I tried. Wherever I was, on my way to school, in the classroom, returning from school, in the village shop, in the basement with Abortus, at home, Eve's image never left me. It was imprinted in the folds of my brain. Mother followed the strange twitching of my face with growing alarm. Whatever I spoke of, my face was always set at a grin and hardly ever in tune with what I was saying. One day I was telling her about the boy in my class who drowned after being pushed into a ground hole containing quicklime, but all the time there was a smile on my face. Mother spoke to Father, insisting that this was definitely a sign of brain damage.

Father rejected her supposition, but failed to offer a viable explanation. I could see that my strange behaviour got him worried, perhaps even more so than Mother. I had no doubt that my Father loved me and would do anything to help me keep sane. He had proved that a number of times, not only by discussing my case with Dr. Kleindienst, but also by denying to the police that he had any idea who might have broken into the surgery. It certainly wasn't me, he insisted. Yes, the ampoules had been found at Grandpa Dominic's house, but I had nothing to do with it. Yes, the girl was an addict, and he gave her maintenance doses whenever she came to visit her grandfather. But he was obliged to do so as a doctor, to prevent her from experiencing a withdrawal shock. Yes, someone had broken into the surgery and stolen the ampoules, but who it was was anybody's guess and for the police to find out. It certainly wasn't me. Much more likely it was the girl herself. In any case her father, who deserves a slap on the face rather than a medal for parenthood, had taken her home now, and that was the end of the matter as far as he was concerned.

Why would my Father lie to protect me if not for the only possible reason that he loved me? He must have known pretty well who the culprit was. Even Abortus agreed with me, when I read him my diary record of events. He must have found the whole thing quite engrossing, because in the end he seemed to be smiling in much the same way I did.

When my grinning became so much a part of me that I wasn't aware of it any more, an event took place which made me realise with a shock that all was not well. One morning at school, during an interval, I bumped into a physics teacher who unexpectedly stepped out of a classroom into the corridor. He slapped my face. Although he was no less astonished at his reaction than I was, I couldn't wait for him to apologise; I ran into the toilet and locked myself in one of the cabins. To suppress the violent sobbing that was rising toward my throat, I stepped out again to walk up and down. One of the taps was dripping and I thought it might be a good idea to splash some water on my face.

There was a mirror above the sink, and no matter how hard I tried to avoid catching sight of my reflection, that was exactly what happened. My chest was nearly bursting with grief, but my face was twisted into the stupidest smile imaginable. Every few moments my mouth would relapse into a pouting expression of torment, but only for a split second, then it would again spread out into a picture of vacant joy and benevolence. Only the eyes never changed, remaining turned inward, as if living a life of their own, unconnected with me.

When the first wave of horror passed, I tried to mobilise my facial muscles to create the expression that would convey my true feelings. But whether I extended or contracted the muscles, the smile would return as soon as I relaxed them. I tried to lengthen the interval between con bouts of smiling, but as soon as I batted an eyelid or twitched the corner of my mouth, the smile would return in spite of my efforts to affect a sombre expression. The pressure in my chest ebbed away and was replaced by a dull burden of humiliation.

I decided to return to the classroom. But in the corridor I realised that I couldn't really do that; I had simply run out of strength to cope with the discomfort of the teachers and the smirking of my schoolmates. I turned and ran down the stairs and out into the courtyard. It was there that I realised I had left my bag in the classroom. But I no longer cared, I ran all the way home, keeping as much as possible to the wood, to meet as few people as possible. I locked myself in my room and decided never to come out again.

Late in the afternoon I smashed the wall mirror and climbed into bed, pulling the duvet over my head. I did that partly to hide and partly to muffle the sounds of Mother's whining and scolding. When she realised that I had locked myself in, she came to bang on the door and demand that I come out.

"Leave him," I heard Father's disgruntled voice, "let him be, for God's sake."

Mother withdrew and did not return. From time to time I heard them talking to each other in the living room, with Father trying to prove a point and Mother crying. Late in the evening, as I cautiously unlocked the door to sneak to the toilet, I found a plate of spaghetti on the doorstep. I ate the food and put the plate back where I found it. The next morning it wasn't there anymore. There was another, with two fried eggs and a piece of bread. Every so often I would hear the creaking of steps in the corridor, as Mother walked up and down, paused at the door every so often and quietly begged me to come out. "Adam, please, say something, let me hear your voice."

She dared not leave the house, she was afraid I might do something to myself. She took indefinite sick leave.

I don't remember how many days I spent in the room. After a while all days merged into one, especially when it started to rain and everything became suffused with damp mist. It was difficult to tell morning from afternoon, the daylight hardly varied. Everything around me had frozen into an endlessly repeating pattern: the cautious creaking of Mother's steps in front of my door, the steady drizzle of rain outside the window, water dripping from trees in the orchard, raindrops bouncing off the fallen leaves on the ground.

The monotony finally sucked me in as if into a swamp. I stopped opening the door and taking in plates of food; I no longer felt hungry. As for thirst, I would open the window every so often and catch into cupped hands some drops of water falling from a leaking gutter. And I stopped sneaking out to the toilet; I peed out of the window. As for the other thing, there was no need; everything in my bowels had come to a standstill.

Then one day it stopped raining, and the heavy clouds began to disperse. They hung about for another two days as if regrouping for a comeback, but eventually the sun broke through and made the air almost vibrate with the cleansed colours of nature. The weather became my great healer, with the sun bouncing off all the surfaces, and flowing among the trees in the orchard like a river of gold. I unlocked the door and ventured out into the courtyard. I sat on a bench near the garage and tried to reconnect with my innermost feelings. The idea of food no longer repelled me; in fact I would have given anything for a piece of Mother's apple pie, my favourite. I mentioned this to Mother in passing, as if the thing was of no consequence, really, but if she did happen to have one ready I wouldn't mind trying a piece. And I mumbled on as if ashamed of expressing a wish that seemed almost childish.

But Mother, delighted with my apparent return to normality, immediately cycled down to the shop to buy the ingredients. Then she set to work and had the pie ready for the oven in half an hour. While waiting for it to be baked she mentioned as if in passing that the weather was just right for a short holiday in the mountains, among the pine forests and meadows, where we could hike at leisure in complete solitude, regaining peace and energy for the school year ahead. We had not been to the mountains for years, she stressed, clinching her case with the least convincing argument. But I felt no resistance to the suggestion; in fact I found the idea of a train journey, and of wandering through pine forests alone, with no one to face or hide from, quite appealing.

Mother pretended not to see the grinning mask on my face. Only Father would gaze at me across the dining table with a look that expressed an equal measure of fatherly concern and professional confusion. At least that's how I remember interpreting what I saw in his eyes, but perhaps, judging by his relentless gaze, there was more: resentment, anger, guilt, all of it mixed into a new, unfamiliar emotion in which I could no longer feel the unconditional affection I had always been sure of. He, too, was of the opinion that a few days in the mountains would do me good.

The next morning Mother began to pack. I watched her movements without fully understanding what they meant, or even realising that they were in any way connected with me. For that reason I did not pay any attention to the fact that she stuffed my suitcase full of clothes, while she herself took no more than a small bag. Before driving us to the station, Father gave her a sealed envelope: he explained that it contained a personal plea to the manager of the mountain resort to take special care of us. I thought this was going a touch too far; since we were neither handicapped nor incapacitated in other ways, we had no right to expect more than other guests. But Mother placed the envelope in her handbag as if entrusted with an important document.

During the train journey I remained detached. I sat by the window. The clatter of wheels underneath the carriage turned the passing landscape into a series of rhythmic waves and hops, with an iridescence of colours and shapes that began to bring to my mind a flux of memories of recent events, especially those at Grandpa Dominic's house. "Whenever you think of me you must smile! That's an order!" It was an order that I found impossible to resist. It was only by smiling that I could remain in touch with the girl who was prepared to take me on a journey into the land of never-encountered bliss; the girl who would forever remain the queen of my dreams.

Mother left me in peace; she was well aware of the risk of upsetting me. She must also have been ashamed of me, for the carriage was filled with a motley collection of passengers most of whom were staring at me quite openly. In the glass-covered photograph affixed to the wall of the opposite bench I occasionally caught sight of my face, especially clearly when the sun dipped behind clouds for a moment or two. It was the face of a circus clown, with the mouth extended and curved upward in the most stupid grin imaginable. My hair, too, had become strangely rebellious, projecting into the air in twisted tufts like the bristles of an old brush. Our fellow passengers in the carriage could be forgiven for thinking that I was a retarded boy who was being escorted by his Mother back to the home for the mentally handicapped.

Ten minutes before we were due to arrive I went to the lavatory. It was small and filthy, and it smelled so badly that I nearly fainted.

Then I noticed a small mirror above the sink. I was shocked to discover that my face had gained an unhealthy red, almost crimson colour, and was developing gaps, not only in the skin, but in the flesh, too, and that these gaps were growing as fast as I could follow the process with my eyes. The smile was no longer the problem; suddenly, something worse appeared to be happening. I began to feel very hot all over my body, as if blood had started to boil in my veins, and I was assailed by the fear of losing my face. I utilised all my remaining strength to get away from the mirror, I even forgot the pressure in my bladder which had brought me there, but some devilish force kept me glued to my reflection: I was obliged to watch how parts of my face vanished before my eyes.

First the hair disappeared as if melting away, and my scalp turned shiny white; then a dark hollow appeared in my forehead, or, to put it more accurately, the hollow did not appear *in* my forehead but simply replaced it; then my lower jaw began to wobble and melt like butter in a hot frying pan. Then, one after another, the remaining parts of my face disappeared; they did not fall off or crumble, they simply paled and sank into themselves, became less and less visible, until they turned into vibrating air. In the end only eyes remained on top of the brain stem jutting out from my trunk, large, wide-open, tear-swollen eyes.

20

No one ever told me how I managed to get from the filthy train lavatory to the bottom of the wide stairs which leading up to the entrance of the mountain resort. A golden October afternoon was sinking into the embrace of a chilly evening above the roof of the imposing building, which looked more like a palace than a mountain holiday home. Below me, the gilded woods of birch and elm cascaded into the valley like a sea of colour which an earthquake had turned into a huge waterfall. Wherever I looked, whether at the cool sky or the leaf-strewn lawns in front of the building, I felt creeping anxiety which made me dizzy.

"Adam," Mother took me by the elbow and pulled me towards the entrance. "They're waiting for us."

No one was waiting for us, quite the contrary: we had to march up and down long corridors for almost an hour, with surly officials sending us from office to office as if this was what they were being paid for, and everywhere Mother protested, complaining that she could not understand how things could have gone so horribly wrong after the place had been so clearly reserved. In the end it was all sorted out and we got a nice room with a view of the cascading woods and the valley bellow. But the room was too small for both of us, it had only one, very narrow bed, so Mother said that she would get another room for herself, I should unpack and relax, and we would see each other at breakfast.

Why not at dinner, I wanted to ask, but Mother's steps had already drawn away down the corridor. I saw her neither at dinner nor at breakfast the following morning, and not even at lunch. I did not see her at all, and when I asked what they had done with her I was told that she had gone home. This was confirmed by the manager of the holiday home, who called me into his office and spent quite a long time reading Father's recommendation letter. He found parts of it so interesting that he went over them twice.

"Well, my goodness," he muttered as he was nearing the end.

He placed the letter into a folder on which someone had already scrawled my name. I had no idea why it was necessary to keep files on the guests of a mountain holiday home, but they were obviously well organised here, and clean, too; why else would many of the staff walk around in white coats. The manager, too, was wearing a white coat, very much like Father's, but for some reason he reminded me more of an assistant in a delicatessen shop, probably because of his rosy, puffed-up face.

"Albert," he gave me a superficial smile. Then his eyes were drawn to the name on the folder. "Sorry, Adam. You are Adam, aren't you?"

I nodded.

"Let me tell you what we're going to do, Adam. We're going to wipe that smile off your face. And then, if you allow me a little pun, you'll be able to go home with a smile on your face. What?" And he laughed, expecting me to do the same.

"But I don't have a face anymore," I said.

I told him briefly what happened on the train.

He pushed back his chair, rose to his feet and beckoned me to follow him to the mirror on the side wall next to the door. "Come, come," he became impatient.

I joined him in front of the mirror, but dared not look into it; the thought of what I might see was enough to make me feel weak in the knees. But the manager placed his hand under my chin and jerked my head upward; before I could close my eyes I caught sight of my face in the mirror, and, miraculously, my face was again in its place, completely normal, fully restored, including the smile, which had become an inseparable part of me.

"You don't have a face?" the manager asked.

I explained that for some inexplicable reason it had come back.

"There you are," he said. "You've only just arrived, and already we're noting improvements. The mountain air appears to be good for you."

That may have been so, but certainly not with regard to some other guests, who appeared to be in a far worse state than I. If they didn't emit piercing shrieks or bang on the walls, they would stand around like statues, staring into the air or at the floor in front of their feet. Some of them never got out of their pyjamas, and not once did I see anyone setting off for a walk in the woods, a normal sight in mountain holiday homes. Some walked up and down, engaged in endless arguments with themselves, while others crawled around on all fours as if looking for a lost button. Very few guests behaved as if they were on holiday.

There were two wings on our floor, one for men and the other for women. This was another thing that seemed out of place. Surely there should have been some married couples there, and some families with pre-school children. There were none. This was most unusual. When, at breakfast, I mentioned my doubts to an unkempt girl who amused herself by throwing porridge all over the floor, she shrieked:

"This is not a holiday home, you dummy! This is a home for people who have gone bonkers. What's wrong with you? Haven't you been to mental gymnastics?"

Mental gymnastics, as it was called, began on the third day after my arrival. I was taken to a special room and asked to lie down on a narrow table. There followed a routine medical examination of the kind I had seen Father do hundreds of times: they took my blood pressure, listened to my heart, measured my lung capacity, shone a small light into my throat and asked me to say "aaahhr". When satisfied that I wasn't dying of a mysterious illness, they wedged a thick stick of firm rubber between my teeth. They pressed my hands to my body and strapped me to the table so hard that I could not move. Then they attached small receivers to my temples, as if they were about to play me some music. The man who appeared to be in charge, asked for my name.

"Right, Adam," he said. "Close your eyes and imagine you're walking through a pleasant wood."

Later I tried to record the details of this pleasant walk in the notebook I had been given, and in which I had been asked to write down anything that occurred to me, dreams, passing thoughts, opinions, whatever. I realised that I could not remember a single thing, except for a sudden blow to my head and the burning heat that immediately followed. The rest was blankness.

Mental gymnastics was then repeated every third day, but in the meantime there were other developments. They began to give me pills; every day at nine, one and six o'clock I had to swallow with a full glass of water two pinkish tablets. At first I protested, explaining that I had neither a headache nor any other condition that would warrant medical treatment, but gradually, feeling that the pills made me less anxious, I began to look forward to these daily rituals, even asking for a higher dose, which I was denied. I began to notice that Eve was no longer in my thoughts all the time; the smile on my face was slowly loosing its grip. The manager's prediction had begun to come true earlier than expected.

Every morning at ten I was called into a little room where a man and a woman asked me questions and recorded my answers in little notebooks. They asked me about school, Mother, Father, Eve. The books I had read. About my interests, and what made me happy. But above all they wanted to know about dreams. When they began. How long they usually lasted. Are there dreams in which I realise I'm dreaming? Do I ever start dreaming on purpose? Can I decide to wake up while dreaming?

The woman wanted to know if any objects or animals appeared in my dreams. I told her about chickens, eggs, rooster, human bone, a snake, a frog-like being on an oak leaf, the dark-haired girl and her pretty blond friend. I mentioned that Father and I entered one particular dream together. I did not say a word about Abortus. Nor did I mention Father's bonsai. I spoke only about what I felt could be dreams. And about what I knew were dreams. The man wanted to know to what extent dreams about Father and Eve differed from one another. How they started. Where I normally found myself when I woke up. Did I find them exciting? Did I ever wish they would come back while I was awake? Could I live without them?

In a few days they were joined by another man, much older, white-haired, slightly stooped and grumpy. His questions were insolent and I refused to answer most of them. Had I ever seen Mother's sexual organ? Had I ever caught Mother and Father making love? Do I ever dream about Mother? When did I start masturbating, and how often do I do it? Who do I love more, Mother or Father? Do I hate Mother? Would I prefer Father to live with another woman? Am I afraid of death? How do I imagine my future? Do I think I am more intelligent than my school mates? Had I ever taken any drugs. Do I ever think about suicide? How would I describe life, ugly or beautiful?

And so on, day after day. Some things I told them many times over. Some they could not get out of me. About some I lied. I was not convinced by their assurances that they merely wanted to help me. I felt they were burrowing into me for their own amusement, or because they were obliged to by the rules of their work. They did not really care about what would become of me. For them, I was just a case, and by the look of it a very interesting one, for the number of people who wanted to interview me steadily grew. Some even came from the city in large gleaming automobiles; I could see them parking in front of the building. And when they finished their conversations with me, they did not leave straightaway, they would hang about in front of the building, exchanging views, gesticulating wildly and defending God knows what points of view.

My diary, in which I was supposed to "free-associate", as they called it, remained almost empty, for mental gymnastics had slowed down my thoughts to such an extent that I could record no more than occasional flashes from "the unconscious", for example, "I hover above the waterfall of the golden sea of autumn which refuses to tumble me into the depths in which alone my wishes might be fulfilled", or, "the sky above the mountain resort watches me with the silent sadness of a mariner deprived of his boat", or, "when I finally sail across the sea of memories, no trace of me will remain anywhere".

My examiners pounced on these words as if they represented the first glimmer of hope that my problem may one day be solved. What exactly did I mean by the mariner deprived of his boat, and what were the wishes I wanted fulfilled? I was becoming very tired, and increasingly reticent and detached; finally I stopped answering altogether. They begged me, threatened me, promised the earth, but I would not budge; I had decided to give them nothing more. There was nothing more; they had cleared me out.

So it seemed like a waste of time when the manager of the mountain resort, in whom after two weeks I still could not see the head of a psychiatric hospital, announced that he had organised a small conference of specialists who would look at my case from all possible angles. As far as I was concerned their angles had nothing to do with me, but the manager insisted that it was very important to arrive at a diagnosis; especially now that the treatment had been going on for some time. Extra chairs were brought to his office, enough to accommodate eight invited specialists in diseases of the mind, and some students and house doctors. All in all enough people to make me feel like an exotic parrot whose feathers had to be plucked one by one to see if the parrot's itching was caused by bedbugs or lice.

It was ten in the morning and the sun was shining through the window straight into my face, lighting it up for interrogation. I was perching on an uncomfortable chair next to the rear wall, where I had been placed on display, so that those gathered would not mistake me for one of their own. The manager sat at his desk on my left, with the expectant audience of know-it-alls spread out in front of the window, with their faces in the shade. I could feel their eyes on me, so I closed mine to avoid meeting theirs even by chance; I could always say that I was bothered by the sun. And so, with eyes closed, I spent the greater part of their discussion of my "hypertrophic dreams". The definition was Father's, but the gathered experts had obviously failed to come up with a better one.

After all these years my memory of that meeting is still surprisingly clear. Although I had only come to understand certain expressions and phrases through my prolific reading later on, I can say with some certainty that I had been forced to listen to a lot of animated drivel about archetypes and symbols, analogies between my dreams and ancient myths, suppressed sexual leanings towards my Father, which in my dreams I conveniently projected onto a pretty young girl, and the like. I had to listen to lengthy arguments in support of the view that most, if not all, objects in my dreams, the snake, human bone, frog-head and especially the rooster had phallic connotations, and that my dreams were quite clearly an expression of my inferiority complex with regard to my schoolmates, for they represented at least one domain which was mine alone, and in which I was the undisputed king. I had to listen to emphatic propositions about the possibility of addiction to erotic images, which might not be dreams at all, but daydreams, for how could they be dreams, since not a single such case had been registered in the whole of psychoanalytic literature!

One of the invited experts spoke about my neurosis as being the consequence of an exaggerated care of my Mother, who probably enjoyed an unsatisfactory love life with my Father, and so projected all her love and care onto her son, without letting him grow up and free himself from her influence. This meant that the only way the son could escape her was through dreams, in which he was punishing the possessive Mother by betraying her, not alone, of course, but by using his father as a proxy, the very one who, with his denial of love and support, had forced Mother into the role of Jocasta in the first place. And so on, all spoken in earnest and with true scientific zeal. I did not catch everything, because in between I managed to doze off a number of times.

My attention intensified only once: when one of the invited guests, a young man who looked like a student, although the others referred to him as doctor, unfolded colour photocopies of what he called two major works of art. The first one, from he seventeenth century, was painted by Hendrick Sorgh. The picture showed a man sitting at a table and playing the lute, with a dog lying at his feet and gnawing a bone. The painting was realistic, finished to the smallest detail, with all parts of the composition clearly recognisable.

The other painting was created by Joan Miró and represented some sort of artistic plagiarism, with the components of Sorgh's picture shifted into a completely different, surrealist style. Everything that Sorgh painted was still there, but broken up into colour fragments, with the lute player having no torso, the dog much smaller, and the lute having the shape of an unfamiliar animal; in other words, reality had evaded the rules of ordinary perception and moved into the realm of imagination and dreams.

Something similar, continued the young doctor, had happened to me. I no longer perceived reality the way it was perceived by the author of the first painting, and was perceived by and large by everybody else. I perceived it more the way it was perceived by the author of the second painting, with shapes and meanings and events slightly out of focus or in double focus. The question, therefore, is not whether I keep having the same dreams all the time, the question is whether my dreams are dreams at all, or perhaps reality which is so shocking that I can only absorb it Miró-like, transfigured into dream images, which on the one hand I probably find sexually exciting, while on the other I am released from any blame for what I dream about. This could also be more than a credible explanation for why my dreams appear so tenacious.

The next question, perhaps even more important, is the nature of my shifts from one type of reality to another: to what extent am I aware of them, to what extent do I control them, and how great is the danger that both of these pictures will join into one, which will be neither the first nor the second, but a third – a mature psychosis. This, concluded the young doctor, is what we should talk about, not about Freud's phallic symbols or Jung's mysticism.

He rolled up the two paintings and quietly returned to his chair. There was a silence. Then it came like a landslide; it sounded as if he had been pounced on by everybody at the same time. I was overcome by complete exhaustion, I don't remember whether I fainted or fell asleep, but the last thing I recall was slowly sliding off the chair onto the floor, from where I must have been carried to my room, where I later awoke in my bed.

A look out the window told me that evening was not far away. The cascading woods were suddenly very dark, as if the trees had lost all their leaves in a single day. Darkness was creeping up from the valley, from down below and from somewhere inside me, slowly, inexorably. For the first time I began to suspect that I was seriously ill. And for the first time since coming to the mountain holiday home I felt desperately lonely, wanting to return home.

I dared not even think that this could ever happen, at least not for many years. But only three days later I was summoned to the manager's office. He wanted to know how I was. I said I was a little tired, but otherwise quite all right; mental gymnastics must have done me a lot of good.

"I'm glad to hear that," he said rather cagily, as if not completely convinced I was telling the truth. "What about dreams?"

"Dreams?" I asked. "What dreams?"

He looked at me as if I were playing some childish game.

"Dreams because of which you are here, boy," he said with a touch of impatience.

"I've stopped having them, sir."

"What do you mean, you've stopped having them?"

I shrugged. "Those dreams stopped as soon as I came here."

"Just like that?"

"Just like that, sir. You said yourself that the mountain air was very healthy."

He winced. "Are you making fun of me?"

"Not at all, sir."

And I shook my head vigorously.

"Why didn't you say so before?"

"No one asked me, sir," I said quietly, secure in the knowledge that I was telling the truth.

"Your smile is gone, too," he said approvingly. After a short reflection he added, "Almost no reason for you to stay any more."

"No, sir," I nodded, making sure I did not sound too eager.

For a few moments he drummed with his fingers on the table. Then he opened my file and wrote something on a sheet of paper.

"Well," he said with a smirk of satisfaction, "we're continuously reproached that we don't really cure anybody." He crossed his arms and smiled at me almost gratefully. "Hardly so, is it, Albert?"

"Adam," I said.

21

It was All Saints' Day when I left the "home for people who have gone bonkers". The train was almost empty, so I stretched out on the bench and dozed off, waking just in time to alight at the right station. I looked around for Father, who was supposed to pick me up, but he wasn't there; he must have been held up by an urgent case. I thought of telephoning him from the nearby inn, but just before reaching the entrance I turned and walked past it. The telephone was probably at the bar, the waiter and other guests would overhear the conversation, and I simply had no strength for exposing myself like that. The simplest thing was to walk home through the woods.

A light drizzle soon turned to rain, and as I walked among the trees with an umbrella in my left hand and my suitcase in the right, water soon penetrated my shoes, which began to make squishy noises. I listened to the rustling of fallen leaves under my feet, but the sound was not harsh, it was dull and soft, which I found comforting. The wood spread around me like a smooth-combed and shivering beast, with branches mutely curved downwards with heavy moisture, and with ominous shadows lurking in the depth of its eyes. It seemed to be afraid of me, an old acquaintance whose footsteps were suddenly so much slower, stickier and more careful than they used to be.

Many reproaches hung in the air between us as I walked through its heart, and both were impatient to part company, since there was nothing we had to say to each other any more. As the trees finally thinned and I noticed a patch of dull sky ahead, we both breathed a sigh of relief. Before continuing toward the village I turned around and saw the wood regaining some of its old energy, with the tops of trees swaying under a sudden gust of wind. But then, as if aware of my look, the wood sank back into itself, into shivering silence, to hide its feelings of guilt. I looked through the mist of rain to the hills for any signs of light among the clouds, but everything was dark, with the rain falling evenly, in tiny drops. There was no indication that the weather would change, although it was All Saints' Day, one of those days when these hills were invariably bathed in cool, clear, fresh-smelling sunshine.

When I reached home I was completely drenched. Father was at the surgery, Mother was in the kitchen, preparing lunch.

"Oh," she said, looking at me through the door, "you're wet." Then she carried on with the cooking.

The house was filled with the smell of chrysanthemums. I thought I could also smell incense, the kind used in Catholic churches, which was unusual, because I knew there wasn't any. But the smell of chrysanthemums always reminded me of cemeteries, death, funerals, and incense appeared to be an integral part of it. The floor had been vacuumed, the curtains had been washed, and everything was in its place. A smell of roast pork was wafting through the open door of the kitchen. These were reliable signs that the day was not ordinary, but a holy day, which on Mother's insistence had to be different, always smelling of something saintly, dark, and unusual.

I went to my room, got out of my clothes, took a shower, dressed again and lay down on the bed, staring at the ceiling without any particular thoughts until Mother called me to the dining room. We ate alone; Father was already on the doorstep when he was called back to attend to a girl with a twisted ankle. I was afraid Mother would want to know how it was at the "home for the people who have gone bonkers", but fortunately she showed no interest in that at all, or in anything else for that matter. She used her right hand for eating, and her left hand for holding the book she was reading, one of those chatty, long-winded books about romantic entanglements in exotic places, the only kind of books she read.

In the afternoon we walked to the cemetery. It was still raining. Father was wearing a black hat, a little too small for the size of his head, and a coat which he could not button up so that it flapped around him, especially as the wind grew stronger. Umbrellas soon became useless, we were soaked to skin, and Mother began to complain that she had water in her shoes and would catch pneumonia for sure. In the cemetery, which was on a steep slope, soil had already turned to mud, especially at the lower end, where water had been accumulating since early morning, and we had to tread carefully to avoid slipping.

Then we stood by the graves and waited.

A shy bell began to tinkle in the chapel at the top of the cemetery. While the wind carried its sound this way and that, dark figures stood in groups among the decorated graves, facing the chapel as if waiting for something to happen. Soon a small procession emerged from behind the walls, led by the priest and a small boy who was carrying a cross, and followed by the most devout village women. They all knelt in the mud and prayed, with the dark figures muttering appropriate refrains, which the blustery wind immediately muffled, so that they never reached the top of the slope. A large flock of ducks flew over us, disappearing in the mist of the falling rain.

"What a day," I heard one of the dark figures say into the wind.

There was a distance between me and the dark figures, although on this particular day we were very much alike, all facing the chapel, all holding large black umbrellas, all standing in mud, all wearing creased and mud-spattered trousers or skirts, all wrapped in ill-fitting, rain-soaked coats or capes or thick winter jackets, all waiting for the ordeal to end. Father, Mother and I were standing at the grave of Mother's parents, almost completely neglected, for the woman Mother used to pay to take care of it had died, and Mother failed to engage another.

Higher up the slope I noticed Grandpa Dominic, leaning on a stick and looking frail, much frailer than ever before, but standing straight as if unwilling to admit to himself and to others that he, too, would soon be lying in a coffin in that wet soil. He was alone, without Eve. Placidly, but with an unbearable burning in my heart, I accepted the fact that I would never see her again. In fact, when I think of it now, the burning was much less unbearable than

I had expected. Something had been killed off in the "home for people who have gone bonkers", some essential part of me. It was easier to live now, but the colour had gone out of life, everything had become grey, monotonous.

When the procession disappeared back into the chapel, the dark figures moved. People were leaving. Candles flickered on most of the graves, covered by makeshift paper umbrellas or encased in small carton boxes, but the flames had a very short life, for the boxes could not withstand the rain for long, or they were blown away by the wind which rolled them about until they were stepped on by shuffling feet and pressed into the mud, or carried, stuck to heels, out of the cemetery. Some people entered the chapel for the final service. Mother did, too. By Father's will we never went to church, but this was the one occasion on which she would not compromise. Father and I slowly walked home.

"Quite chilly," Father said after five minutes, and I replied, "Yes." Those were the only words spoken.

Towards the evening, when Mother finally returned, a quarrel erupted between her and Father. It may have been caused by the tension which was slowly filling the house, or by the desolation of the deserted fields outside, or by the chilly wind rattling the panes in sporadic bursts, dry and biting, for the rain had stopped. Or it may have been the pernicious silence which had enveloped us in the living room, with Father leafing through a medical journal and Mother lying on the sofa and turning the pages of her book without reading it, all the while thinking about something else.

In the end she closed the book and sat up. She began to speak. She spoke in her usual haughty, telling tone which would grate on my nerves and make Father twist his face into a tortuous grin.

How could I do this, she asked. How could I bring such shame on her, not only at school and in the village, or in front of her relatives, but also, more importantly, in front of Father's patients? For years he had been trying to strengthen his reputation, but now, just as he had managed to register his 499-th patient, one short of half a thousand, the first three hundred will stop coming because the doctor's son had gone mad! Who is going to retain trust in his abilities after this? Do I realise that I had begun to destroy what used to be one of the most respected families for miles around, and which is now in such straits that even the Gypsies enjoy greater respect?

I gave Father an imploring look.

At first he averted his eyes as if embarrassed. Then he closed his journal and quietly asked Mother to stop mouthing inanities. Mental illness is not a matter of choice, like taking heroin, smoking or drinking, which anyone with sufficient will can give up. Nor, speaking of it, is mental illness the same as popping pills for every little twinge in the body or mind. When will she stop removing antibiotics, tranquilisers and other dangerous drugs from the dispensary without first getting a doctor's prescription?

This was enough to get Mother to her feet and into a flaming rage.

"You," she pointed her finger at him, "you are responsible for all this. You encouraged him to dream about that little slut, you said this was part of his growing up – what Father on earth would ever say that? And now she is here again, I saw her on the way home. You, yes, *you* did everything to drive your son crazy."

"What do *you* know?" Father struck back with all his authority. "What do *you* know about the human psyche and its mysteries, about the inner landscapes you don't even know exist, let alone be able to visit them in your dreams?"

He got to his feet and folded the journal as if about to swat a fly.

"What do *you* know," he continued, "about the solitary places in the soul, where desires change into vultures, and where your own shadow is trying to strangle you with every step you take? What do *you* understand, with the horizon you possess? Don't you realise that dreams are a universe into which we must propel ourselves with the full force of intellectual power, if we are to explore it?

"If you don't leave him alone," Mother took a step toward Father, "I shall report you to the Medical Association. God is my witness. I will ask them to examine your head. I'll go to the police and tell them that you're deliberately driving your own child crazy. And don't think – "

She could not finish the sentence, for Father took a step toward her and struck her on the face with the folded journal. The blow dislodged her spectacles, which fell to the floor, bounced a few times and ended in front of my feet, with one of the lenses broken. I picked them up and felt the shattered lens with my fingers. I must have pressed on it too hard, for the lens disintegrated, with the bits landing on the floor. Father and Mother stared at me as if trying to apportion the blame for what happened to me.

Then Mother distorted her face as if trying to quell a surge of tears welling up inside her. She rushed into the hall and hastily put on her coat.

"You're never going to see me again," she hissed at us venomously. She slammed the door behind her. I ran to the window and looked out. I saw her cycling furiously down the driveway toward the road.

"Mother!" I called weakly.

"Let her be," Father said grumpily. "Didn't you see she left with slippers on? She'll be back. Much too soon."

22

Late at night I was suddenly thrown out of sleep; it seemed to me that someone was quietly calling my name. I listened intently, but all I could hear was my breathing. Just as I was about to sink back into sleep, someone rapped on the window pane and a mysterious voice whispered my name. I pressed my face against the cold glass. At first all I could see were the stars, the moon and the sharply delineated shadows of trees. Even a few moments later, as my eyes got used to the conditions outside, I could see nothing more than the bare orchard and the silhouette of the wood in the background. The whole thing must have been an illusion. I decided to climb back under the duvet, it was cold.

Just then a figure appeared among the trees in the orchard, and moved slowly toward the window. As it left the region of the shadows I could see clearly that it was a young woman with a mane of black hair, which was falling over her shoulders. She was wrapped from head to toe in a grey blanket, but barefoot. She seemed to be smiling at me. As she came right up to the window, I recognised her. It was Eve.

With a quick movement she drew the blanket apart. She was completely naked. In the moonlight her body appeared to be softly rounded and more enticing than ever. I was assailed by feelings I had never experienced before: cold and heat spread through my veins in simultaneous waves, making me glow and shiver. With the last vestiges of reason I tried to find an explanation for why she had come. She might have come in the hope that I would once again get those ampoules for her. Or she might have come for a less selfish reason: to enter with me into that dream she had promised me. Or both. Or just to say hello to me, which seemed unlikely. But none of this really mattered. The only thing that mattered was that she was there, in front of the window, smiling at me.

Was she really there, or was the whole thing again only a dream? I pinched both my ears, and the pain was sufficiently pronounced to make it unlikely that I was dreaming. Then again, in many of my dreams things had remained as real, or become even more so than in a waking state. To make doubly sure I wasn't dreaming I banged my head against the wooden frame of the window. This time there was no doubt that I was awake, and that Eve was real, and that she had come for me. But why was she wearing a black wig?

Without any further misgivings I opened the window, climbed onto the sill and jumped out into the orchard. Eve had already moved away and was beckoning me with a curved forefinger to follow her. As I moved, barefoot and wearing only pyjamas, across the shadows spread out on the cold, dewy ground, she floated away towards the edge of the wood, light as a fairy. I ran after her as hard as I could, but she kept evading me, flickering through the moonlit wood like a large moth, turning every time she emerged into a clearing to wave me on. At first I did not feel any cold, but soon the chill of the November night began to bite. Gradually, my elation began to subside, giving way to a strange premonition that this midnight pursuit through the woods would not end well. My fear became even more pronounced as we reached an intersection of two forest paths, where Eve took the left one, which led toward the edge of the forest and across the meadows into the village. Again she turned and beckoned me to follow.

But something forced my eyes to the right, along the path which led through a thicket of bushes and newly planted pines to the main road. Not far away, standing in the middle of the path, was a human figure staring in my direction. I froze. Cold sweat broke out on my forehead. I could see Eve drawing away to the left. At the same time the figure on the right began to move towards me. I could not move, I was stuck to the ground. As the figure emerged into a patch of moonlight my fear turned to horror: walking toward me, leaning on her bicycle, was Mother. I could even hear the familiar creaking of the rusty axle of the front wheel. Soon she was standing right next to me. Her eyes were red from intense crying, and filled with hatred. She was wearing the slippers in which she had stormed out of the house the previous evening.

I looked to the left and saw that Eve was already far away, still beckoning me to follow. I gathered all my strength and began to run. Mother climbed on her bicycle and pedalled after me; I could tell by the creaking of the axle that she was gaining on me. Another few moments, and she was cycling alongside me. She began to speak. The tone of her voice was unlike any I had heard before; it was ugly, crow-like and threatening. She was saying that she had finally caught me red-handed, right in the middle of contemplating an indecent act that would bring even greater shame on our family. This she could not allow. If I turned back now and went home with her, she would forgive me, and no more would be said about it. If I didn't, I would have only myself to blame for the consequences.

I said nothing, my lungs were nearly exploding with the effort I was putting into the running. I wanted to call to Eve to wait for me, for she was already getting lost in the darkness, but I was so out of breath I couldn't utter a single word. Then I saw the bicycle shooting ahead. Mother had started to pedal furiously to catch up with Eve.

"No!" I shouted after her. "No!"

But she refused to listen. We left the wood behind and were crossing meadows and fields, with the village on the other side of the stream. I could just see Eve floating across the foot-bridge, looking back and gesturing to me to hurry up. Mother was right behind her, I could see her lifting the bicycle and carrying it across to the other side of the stream. Then she bent down and, with the strength I would never have thought she had in her, lifted the footbridge, which consisted of a single planed trunk of a pine tree, and tossed it into the stream, causing a splash. She straightened up and waited for me like a stern schoolteacher for a pupil who has to be punished for a grave misdemeanour.

I stopped on the bank of the stream. I realised that only half a mile further up was the dam on which everything had begun. And it suddenly struck me that it could all have been so different. If it had been raining that afternoon, or Eve had not come to sunbathe, or Father had not discovered us on the dam, my dreams might never have started. And if they hadn't, would I now be standing where I was? Would anything that was behind me have happened at all? Most probably my life and my future would have turned out completely different. But I could also feel that back-tracking was impossible, and that there are moments in life when by a single, seemingly insignificant move or decision one's destiny is sealed, determining one's actions for years to come.

So it seemed useless to resist the urge that drove me on. The stream was not very deep, I could wade or even swim across, but the water must have been freezing cold. From the other side Mother hissed towards me not to attempt to cross, because she would have no choice but to drown me. A strange emotion suddenly rose from the depths of my being, something that had been lying there for a long time. I did not care any more what I did, as long as I got past Mother to reach what belonged to me, more than to anyone in the world.

I jumped into the stream and waded across. The icy water sank its teeth into my skin like a ravenous wolf. But I ignored the cold, sudden hatred had given me back all my strength. As I tried to climb out onto the opposite bank, Mother kept slapping my fingers with the hard heels of her slippers, hitting me on the head with her hands, and pushing me back into the freezing water. All my attempts to crawl out ended in failure. The cold and the effort soon made me dizzy.

In a moment of despair, when I no longer knew what I was doing, I fetched a sharp stone from the bottom of the stream and tossed it at Mother's head with all the force I could muster. The stone hit her in the forehead and made her collapse with a cry of shock. Her inattention gave me just enough time to climb out of the water and hurry on after Eve, who was waiting for me on the outskirts of the village. Afraid that I would lose her, I ran as fast as I could, waving my arms and shouting, "Wait, wait."

The creaking of the axle soon told me that Mother had recovered and was right behind me. It wasn't long before she streaked past me, bent over the handlebars, with her jaw grimly jutting out before her, legs pumping furiously. Soon she was far ahead, disappearing among the houses, closely on the heels of Eve. Expecting the worst, I ran even faster and did not stop until I reached the village chapel, where I had to decide whether to continue up the road, which was one way to Grandpa Dominic's house, or across the cemetery and down the slope, which was another, shorter way.

I had no doubt that Eve, especially with Mother in hot pursuit, would have chosen the shortcut. I ran up a small incline to the cemetery. Sure enough, the first thing I noticed was the bicycle which Mother had leant against the wall of the chapel. The small wooden gate which led to the cemetery was open. I ran through it, and down among the graves. Mother was waiting for me. She was standing in the middle of the path which was cutting the cemetery in two. In the moonlight I could clearly see that she was tightly gripping the crossbar of a wooden cross. She must have wrenched it off a cross on one of the graves. Behind her, lower down, I saw Eve, who was still frantically gesturing me to follow her.

I was completely exhausted. All I was really aware of was my desire to reach her at any cost. I was prepared to remove or destroy anything standing in my way. First I tried to sneak past Mother, believing that she would not try to hurt me. But she raised the crossbar and hit me on the back so hard that I fell to my knees. When I managed to rise, she was standing before me as impervious as before, with her feet apart, immovable as a column of stone.

"Help!" I shouted. "Father, help me!"

But the sound remained locked inside me; not a word came out of my mouth.

"Mother?" I tried. "Mother, let me pass, please."

This time, too, there was no sound; as if my words had sunk to my stomach or through my veins into the ground below. Suddenly the earth all around trembled and moved. A crowd of snowy-white skeletons rose from the graves and made a circle around us. As they moved, their bones clattered like loose roof tiles in a strong wind. Although they were eyeless, they seemed to be watching us. One stepped out of the group and moved toward me. On the way he bent down, detached his shinbone and pressed it into my hand. His jaw bones moved as if he wanted to give me an encouraging smile.

I gripped the unexpected weapon with both hands. Mother and I attacked each other. The struggle was very short. I hit her over the head; the blow was so powerful that she limply sank to the ground. I kept hitting her with the bone until I broke her skull, disfigured her face and lacerated her limbs. Even when she was already dead I could not stop bringing the bone down on her lifeless body. In the end I threw the blood-spattered weapon among the graves and breathed a sigh of relief. The skeletons clattered; it seemed that they were applauding. The one that lent me his shinbone, now picked it up and slotted it back in place. Before rejoining the group, he patted me on the shoulder. I made a step forward and the crowd parted to let me pass. Victorious and free, I walked down the path towards Eve who was waiting for me at the bottom of the cemetery. She was standing there naked, no longer wrapped in her blanket.

I reached out to touch her hand, but as I did so I realised that I was holding the bony hand of a skeleton, which gave off a sickening smell of decay. Its jaws were set at an angle which reminded me of derisive laughter. Then I heard a clattering sound of derision behind me; as I turned I saw the crowd of skeletons slowly moving towards me. I sank to the ground and was rescued by darkness.

When I opened my eyes it was early morning; a grey, misty light was spread over the hills. My first thought was that I had never had such a vivid dream; I could remember every detail. The only unusual thing was that I did not wake up at home in my bed, but in the cemetery, in my pyjamas, lying on the wet grass among the graves. Candles still flickered on some of them, and the chrysanthemums placed in stone vases the day before still gave off their saintly smell. I felt cold and started to shiver. I noticed strange filth stuck to my sleeves and trouser legs, a mixture of mud, soil and blood. This was indeed the most unusual dream; never before had it happened that I would be carried like a moonwalker to the location of my dream. I ran home across the fields and through the wood, to avoid early risers.

Some time later Father found me in the bathroom, where I was trying to brush traces of what looked like blood off the tips of my fingers. I had no idea how blood could have appeared on my fingers, having only got hurt in a dream, probably while I was trying to climb out of the stream and Mother kept hitting me with her slippers. Everything that had happened in my dream after that point, had already vanished in a blur that meant nothing at all.

I was sitting in the bathtub, rubbing the tips of my fingers with a hard brush. Although the suspicious traces had been rubbed off, I kept brushing the fingers, afraid that they might reappear. My filthy pyjamas were lying on the floor of the bathroom; they were the first thing Father noticed as he entered.

"How are you, Adam?" he asked. He looked very grave; he seemed to have aged by at least twenty years.

"I'm taking a bath," I said, "but I probably won't go to school, I don't feel well."

Father sat down on the edge of the bathtub and looked at me. In his eyes I noticed something I had not seen before, a shadow of great sadness, perhaps disappointment; in any case something that hurt me deeply. As if Father was no longer on my side, as if I had done something that had forever set us apart.

"Mother's gone to work?" I asked.

Father said nothing; he just kept looking at me.

"No," he said after a while, as if waking from a deep thought. "That's what I came to tell you. She had to leave very early, Aunt Yolanda has fallen ill. They phoned late last night."

"When is she coming back?"

After a brief silence he said, "Probably not so soon. Yolanda is her only sister, as you know. She'll probably want to take care of her until she improves. Or dies."

He joined his hands and placed them limply on his knees as if not quite knowing what to do with them. "Remember our common dream?"

I nodded.

He looked at me for a while as if trying to find the right words. Then he said, "I think we should repeat it. I don't mean that particular dream, I mean that we should once again enter a dream together, hand in hand, two souls making a single journey, do you know what I mean?"

I didn't, but I nodded anyway.

He got up, took a towel from a hook on the door and handed it to me with a sense of urgency. "Dry yourself, put some clothes on and come down."

When I entered the living room I found him sitting in the armchair in front of the TV, staring at the blank screen. He didn't notice I had come in.

"Father," I said quietly.

It was only after I called him for the second time that he emerged from his thoughts. He got up immediately and asked me to come to the sofa. He removed a few cushions and pointed to where I should sit. Then he sank his weight into the sofa next to me.

"Adam," he said. "We're going to swallow a dream potion. Then we shall enter a dream in which, with a bit of luck, we shall learn a few important truths. Or sink into darkness from which we shall not rise again. Are you brave enough for this great adventure? Which could well be our last?"

I nodded.

"Are you sure?"

I nodded again. I had nowhere to go, I had nothing to do, and I had no idea what to do with myself. Following Father into a dream, whatever dream, was the only direction left.

"All right, then," he said. "Let's be off."

He reached for the two glasses which were standing on the coffee table and gave one to me, raising the other one to his lips.

"Let's not waste any time," he said. "Ready?"

I nodded.

"One, two, three," he said.

We emptied our glasses with a few gulps. The clear liquid had a bitter-sweet taste, with a touch of something acid, metallic.

23

We were standing on the sea shore and looking toward the horizon. There were no waves. The surface of the sea was smooth and straight, like an endless sheet of grey glass. If we were to roll a marble across it, it would travel unhindered until it bumped against the line of the horizon, where it might bounce off it and travel all the way back. It is normal to see little sailing and other boats off the shore, leaving frothy trails in their wake. But this time there were none. And usually there are other signs of life, such as a dolphin suddenly jumping out of the water and splashing back in. Now there was nothing; dolphins had either left the area or were too frightened to come to the surface.

With good reason, for something was decidedly wrong with the surface of the sea. Father was of the same opinion; I could see that on his face. The sky was clear, the sun was high, but the rays were not reflected by the smooth surface, which was dull and dead, as if the sun was not shining on it at all. But the rocks behind us were shimmering in the sun. It was very hot, with sweat pouring down our faces. I could feel the heavenly fire burrowing into the back of my neck and spreading throughout my body.

I listened carefully for any signs of a breeze that might cool us, but the air was completely still, there wasn't a sound to be heard, most unusual for a summer afternoon on the sea shore. Usually there are waves crashing against the rocks, or, if not, the pine trees sway and rustle in a gentle sea breeze. At the very least you can hear the joyful screams of bathers or music from their transistors radios. This time we could hear nothing at all. The air did not stir, nothing moved.

Then we heard, or thought we heard, something that was definitely close to a sound. Perhaps not quite a sound, more a feeling that something was creeping along. This was the first and only movement we became aware of, but even here we had no idea where it was coming from. All we knew without any doubt was that somewhere close by something was sneakily crawling along. Then we suddenly froze. Peeping out of a hole in the rocks was the head of a snake. It was quite large, of bluish colour, with brown stripes on its back. I couldn't tell whether its eyes were staring at me or at Father. Father thought they were staring at both of us. We did not move. The snake's head bobbed up and down and the reptile began to crawl out of the gap. Its body was thick, smooth and shiny.

Father and I were surprised rather than frightened by the sudden appearance of the strange animal. After all, the snake represented the first sign of life, so our surprise was accompanied by what could almost be called a sense of relief. But this did not last very long, it was suppressed by the obvious fact that it was a snake that was moving, rather than something less dangerous, for example bird, a fish or lizard.

Our visitor, in the meantime, had put its head on the ground and was sliding over the smooth surface of the rock. The snake's body followed its head, emerging through the hole as if unwinding out some underground cave. As the head slowly approached we began to wonder about the snake's intentions. That it was a venomous snake we did not doubt for a moment. It was sliding past approximately a yard from our feet. We briefly hoped that it was sliding to the rocks behind us in order to lie in the sun. Perhaps it wasn't even aware of us. I kept turning my head to follow its progress. So did Father. The snake moved very slowly, as if sliding along required exceptional effort. It must have been incredibly long, for its tail had still not appeared from the hole.

Suddenly the snake turned its head to the left, with its body following in an arc. It occurred to me that she might want to slide around us to reach a flat rocky elevation a little to the left of us, where it would curl up and lie in the sun. I kept turning my head to the left to follow its progress until the snake had crawled so far that my neck began to ache. Then I turned my head in the opposite direction, and soon the snake's head came into view from the right. Father, too, turned his head. The snake had given the flat elevation a miss and was increasingly moving in what looked like a circle. It was sliding back toward the shore, maybe towards some other hole or into the sea. This in itself was not unusual. What couldn't have been coincidence was the obvious and disturbing fact that the snake's distance from our feet was exactly the same all around. The tail had still not appeared from the hole.

Finally the snake managed to get so far that its head was about to slip over the rocky edge into the sea. But instead it turned once again to the left and began to slide toward the gap from which it was still unwinding with the rear part of its body. It was still sliding slowly, evenly, almost deliberately. Now there was no longer any doubt in our minds that it was enclosing us in a circle. This happened a few moments later, when the snake put its head on the rear part of its body and gave us what we could have sworn was a scornful look.

Everything happened so quickly that we could not quite believe the obvious implications. We should have run away as soon as the snake's head appeared from the hole. Then again, how could we have known that the snake had secret plans? Only now could we say with certainty that this was not an ordinary snake, but an evil creature most likely determined to kill us. By exchanging glances Father and I came to the conclusion that we had no choice but to try and escape or let ourselves be killed.

Hand in hand we lifted our left and right feet respectively to make the first leap. But as we did so the snake's head darted into the air and hissed venomously right in front of our faces. We froze. The snake's head withdrew and again came to rest on the rear part of its body, its tiny eyes watching us. Slowly, we lowered our feet to the ground. Now we knew that the snake would kill us the moment we tried to step over its body.

A moment later the snake moved again and began to slide in the same direction as before, equally slowly, the head travelling alongside its body, with more of it coming out of the hole as though there were no end to it, until the head, having made two circles around us, came back to its resting place, from where the snake's tiny eyes watched us no less carefully than before. After a while the snake began to make a third circle around us, this time moving visibly faster, as if wanting to strengthen its ring and finally make our escape impossible. As the ring inexorably widened, we racked our brains for a solution. The snake had encircled us twelve times, and was starting to slide around us for the thirteenth time. The ring of its body was almost two metres wide.

While we marvelled at the unusual capacity of the snake to spread all the way to the horizon, in which case, to escape, we would have to run across its body for many miles, the reptile was making a twenty-second circle. We noticed that its body was getting thinner, and it seemed that we were about to see the end of this incredibly long animal. We did, but instead of the usual tail there appeared another head! The snake had one head at the front and one at the back. One was lying to our left, and the other to our right; whichever way we decided to leap, they would both pounce on us. We had become prisoners of a devious animal whose intentions we failed to interpret correctly.

Suddenly Father spoke. "Adam," he said, "we can't escape this animal. This animal has escaped from us. We have to swallow it and tighten our sphincters so it won't escape ever again."

Although I wasn't quite sure what he meant with his words, they seemed logical: the snake was far more dangerous in a ring around us than it would be in our stomachs, where we could satisfy its hunger by giving it a rat a day. Outside us, it had grown so large that we had become its prey instead.

"Quickly," Father said. "You grab one head, and I'll grab the other."

As soon as we moved, both heads darted into the air and hissed in our faces. We grabbed the snake by its neck, one neck each, pushed its heads into our mouths and began to swallow them. We were swallowing it from both ends at once, watching the ring unwind like the rope of an anchor thrown overboard. The swallowing itself produced no sensations, the snake was merely disappearing; where to, we had no idea, because our stomachs did not swell at all.

In the end we were facing each other with about a yard of the snake's body between us, unable to decide how to share the remainder of the animal which presumably belonged to each of us equally. Suddenly Father decided to swallow the last visible part of the snake as if it belonged to him. As our faces touched, I could feel that he did not stop, but continued swallowing as if obsessed, drawing the part of the snake I had swallowed out of my stomach, either depriving me of my share or taking the burden of playing host to the animal onto himself.

The next moment the dream gradually dissolved into another dream, in which Father and I were lying flat on our stomachs next to each other on a wide table, with our heads hanging over the edge, and with the snake in our mouths no longer thick and scaly, but thin, white and rubbery. In fact we each had a snake of our own now, and both were spouting liquid into a large metal container standing next to the table. Traces of fat and half-digested food were floating on the surface of the liquid already in the container.

Standing behind the container with a funnel in her hand was a woman who strongly resembled Nurse Mary. She was looking at us with a mixture of anger and confusion. The room also appeared familiar; it looked very much like Father's surgery. I heard Father growl, and suddenly the rubber tube began to gag me as well, I felt like vomiting, although there was nothing left in my stomach that could be expelled. My head felt as if it weighed ten stone, I was dizzy and astonished by the sudden move from one dream to another, which was so different from the first.

The next moment the woman who looked like Nurse Mary pulled the tubes from our gullets and asked us to breathe normally.

"Nurse," I heard Father say, "I'll never forgive you. You have no right to make decisions about other people's lives."

"Really?" Nurse Mary affected surprise. "I'm so sorry. I've completely forgotten that only doctors can make decisions about other people's lives. Including, no doubt, the lives of their sons."

"Nor will I ever forgive you your stupid remark," Father tried to raise his voice, but was overcome by weakness and lapsed into silence.

"I don't care," Nurse Mary said and slammed the funnel down on the medicine cabinet. "I have been brought up to believe that lives are sacred, that's why I became a Nurse. Why you became a doctor you had better ask yourself."

She lifted the container with the contents of our stomachs and carried it to the adjoining lavatory. "You're lucky you were discovered by Grandpa Dominic," she said when she came back. "Otherwise you'd now be lying on a different kind of table."

"In that case I hope to see *him* on that table as soon as possible," Father spouted in anger.

"No!" I shouted and began to vomit stomach acid.

"As for me," Nurse Mary said, "I wish this was no more a bad dream."

"It is," Father said. "Only much worse than any of us expected."

24

Soon after these events I slid down the chute into the basement to record the snake dream in my dairy, and to ask Abortus for his opinion. More than ever I felt that I needed advice which would not be confused or approximate, or merely benevolent, like Father's, and which wouldn't simply tell me what was happening, but also what I should do. In the two dreams in which we appeared together, especially the last one, Father had come too close to me; we had become too much like one person, with one pain, one longing, one sense of hopelessness. I felt, not for the first time, but more acutely than ever, that Father, too, needed someone to guide him through a maze of decisions, to tell him what was right and true. That he, too, no less than I, was lost in an emptiness in which there were no signs or pointers, and where he had to decide which direction to take as he went along. It was for that reason that I wanted to record the dream before I forgot any details: to gain, by rereading it later, some sort of understanding of what the dream might have been telling us, for I knew, since reading Jung, even from what little I understood, that dreams were messages from the hidden parts of ourselves to which no access could ever be gained.

Pale sun was shining in through the basement window, so I didn't have to put on the light. The sun was shining directly on Abortus, making him almost transparent. The sunlight also made his eyes appear a lot larger than they were. If he was alive, the expression in his eyes would leave me in no doubt that something terrible must have frightened him. I had no doubt that this was merely a trick of the light, so I did not worry about it; I reached behind the glass jar to pull out my two diaries, *Dreams I* and *Dreams II*. Normally my fingers found them straightaway, but now they scrabbled about in vain. It occurred to me that the last time I might have mistakenly pushed them behind one of the other jars. I checked the entire shelf, reaching behind every jar from both sides. My diaries were not there.

With a heavy heart I sank into myself. Something horrible began to course through my veins, some thick, black, oily blood which the heart refused to suck in and expel on its way through the body. All of it seemed to concentrate in my head, which was getting heavy and dizzy. It was obvious that someone had discovered my *Dreams*, and stolen them.

After that things became a little unclear. I remember sitting on a broken chair and pressing my hands together so hard that my fingers got blue. That must have lasted quite some time, for the beam of sunlight coming in through the window had moved from the shelves to a stack of framed pictures leaning against the opposite wall. They were paintings of anatomical details of the human body, and for what seemed like ages I stared at colour images of internal organs, stomach, liver, lungs, pancreas, gall-bladder, large intestine, but above all the heart which gave the impression that someone had torn it from the chest of a still living being and neatly sliced it in two on a chopping board.

Was it Father who stole my *Dreams*? It could hardly have been anyone else; only he had access to the basement. It must have happened while I was away at the "home for those who have gone bonkers". Now he knew everything about me, every secret thought I recorded, every detail of what I wrote about Eve and him, and their doings in my dreams, every wish of mine that Eve would do those things with me, every prayer to God to make Father impotent or castrate him; every wish for him to suffer a stroke. He knew everything I felt about him in my dreams, but nothing about what I thought of him when I was awake: that he was the best Father I could have wished for, that he could have Eve, if he wanted her, although I knew that he didn't, for he was an older man and her doctor, and would have been happy for me to have her, although she was an addict in need of treatment.

It took a while before I realised that I was crying. Through the mist of tears I began to see things slightly blurred, so when the beam of sunlight moved on and brought into view another of Father's bonsai plants, a large box made of five separate sheets of glass, I at first refused to believe that what I saw was really there. I wiped my tears, rubbed my eyes and looked again. Standing in the corner of the basement, amidst the disorder of old medical journals and other rubbish, was a large glass container. Squeezed into it, sitting in a stooped position, with her head pushed down between her breasts to fit the space, was a naked female body. I rose as if in a dream and slowly moved closer. The woman's matted hair was criss-crossed with streaks of coagulated blood. Cuts on her scalp pointed to heavy blows with a sharp object.

I crouched and looked at the woman's face from below. I felt as if a hot meteorite had penetrated my brain and set it alight. Mother's face was still expressing the horror I remembered from the last moments of our fight at the cemetery, when she collapsed under the force of my blows and twitched before me until further blows made her body come to a rest. But that was a dream! This could mean only one thing: that I was still dreaming. That I didn't know how to be awake anymore. That I had been imprisoned by dreams in the same way Father and I had been imprisoned inside a snake ring.

I came to a conclusion: if I smashed the front sheet of glass with my hand and suffered a cut, or even only a graze, I probably wasn't dreaming. Without any further thought I rammed my fist against the glass which shattered with a spine-chilling noise. My fist did not stop until it bounced off Mother's cheek. The first thing I felt in my knuckles was burning pain, then, through the pain, the limpness of Mother's dead skin. As I withdrew the hand I saw that a tiny sliver of shattered glass had penetrated the skin in the hollow between the knuckles of my forefinger and middle finger. I pulled it out, and immediately blood began to ooze from the tiny wound.

"Mother," I whispered. "Mother, can you hear me?"

Her face was pale and twisted into a tortuous grin. My blow had pushed her head up and back against the rear sheet of glass. Her eyelids were wide open and she seemed to be staring at me with an expression of mild astonishment; the warmest, the least censorious look I had ever seen in her eyes.

I was not particularly horrified at seeing Mother dead. I remembered Eve's words that eternity was the only true happiness we could hope for. Nor could I feel any guilt that it was probably me who held the bone which had broken her skull. I still believed that she had no right to come between me and my desires, whether in dream or reality. Also, I felt no particular gratitude to Father for trying to cover up after me. After all, this wasn't the first time that he had tried to protect me. It had always been clear to both of us that I could expect nothing less. Even so, I was in pain, and I didn't know what was causing it.

I looked at the blood still oozing from the cut on my knuckles, and the thought passed my mind that if I allowed it to flow I might eventually bleed to death. This filled me with relief, the kind of relief I had never experienced before. The knowledge that, after all the horrible things which can happen in life, in the end there awaits every one of us a blissful peace in which no answers have to be sought, because there are no questions, made me feel strangely relaxed, almost comfortable. Vaguely, as if a cat had brushed past my ankles, I was touched by a longing for that blissful state.

But there was still something I had to do. I could not leave my little brother alone with our Mother's body, which was too large to be preserved in formaldehyde and would soon start to decompose (although Father might have brought her to the basement to preserve her as soon as he managed to get a large enough jar). One way or another, I would no longer be coming to the basement, so I had to rescue Abortus and take him home to my room, where I could be with him for all time. As I carefully lifted the jar off the shelf, he swayed in the liquid as if flailing about in sudden fear. Perhaps he knew that he was about to go on a journey, the first after his birth.

I could see at once that it wasn't going to be easy to get the jar up the chute and out into the open. Climbing out required the use of hands as well as knees. If I held the jar in front of me, I could loose my grip on the slippery surface and slide all the way back. If I landed on the chair I needed to reach the chute, the jar could easily break, and that would mean that I had killed not only my Mother but my little brother as well. I had to avoid the possibility of that happening at all costs. If only I had brought my school bag with me; then I could have placed the jar inside it, fully extended the shoulder strap, placed it round my neck and crawled out like that, with Abortus on my back.

I rummaged among the dusty clutter lying about. It wasn't long before I found a length of rope and a large towel, which was covered in filth and mould, but that was immaterial for my purpose. I spread the towel on the ground, placed the jar with Abortus in the middle of it, joined the four corners of the towel above the jar and tied them together first with one end of the rope, then with the other. I placed the rope round my neck from behind, and so the towel became a bag in which I transported Abortus up the chute on my back.

Once outside, I was faced with the question of how to get him home. I decided to keep the jar in the towel. I grabbed the rope with both hands and pulled it a little away from my neck, so it wouldn't suffocate me. And so, with the unusual load on my back, I walked first down the main road and then up the side road to our house. I met quite a few people, who stared at me, turned and followed me with their eyes, even shouted something, but nothing reached me, I did not care, it was just Abortus and me. All the way, inaudibly, just by moving my lips, I kept telling him not to be afraid of being bounced up and down, that we would soon be safely at home.

When we reached the house, I put him on the kitchen table and unwrapped the jar. I took the towel and the rope to the metal rubbish container in front of the house and pushed them under some discarded clothes. I had already let the lid drop when something made me lift it once more. The clothes were Mother's, skirt, blouse, cardigan, panties, bra, stockings, and coat. And slippers. On the coat, blouse and skirt I could see traces of blood and dirt.

I closed the container and returned to the kitchen. It was only now that I realised with a shock that, during my walk home, formaldehyde in the jar had become so cloudy that I couldn't see Abortus at all. Nor was he able to see out. He was surrounded by a muddy liquid which had lost all transparency, and my first thought was to pour it out and replace it with clean water. But the jar was tightly shut with a large cork. Besides, water from the tap might not be the best environment for someone who had spent fifteen years in formaldehyde. I decided to wait for the cloud to settle and the liquid to clear.

I lifted the jar and carried it to my room. I placed it on the cabinet in which I kept my school books and music cassettes, which I had not listened to once since the beginning of summer. I lay down on the bed, joined my hands behind the back of my head, and stared at the fuzzy home of my little brother without once averting my eyes. I decided to wait for the liquid to clear, so I could once again see the frog-like face of my dearest, my only friend.

I joined my hands in front of my chest, closed my eyes and said, "God, if this is a dream, I want to wake up."

Then I said, "God, if this is real, I want to start dreaming."

There was no sign that God had any intention of responding. We never went to church, although it was not far away, on top of the hill above our house. Every Sunday we would see people passing our house on the way to morning mass, and then home again, we would listen to the sound of the bells. We would often pass the church on our way somewhere else, but we never set foot inside. I never asked myself why; that's how it was decided by Father and Mother. Father lived in a world of science and, I am sure of that now, great unhappiness. Mother lived largely in a world of general disapproval of things. I lived in a world of my own. God lived somewhere else. But never before had I felt such a burning desire for him to pass by my window. And knock on the pane. And spend a moment with me.

I looked out the window and saw a patch of pale blue November sky. Winter was not far away, and I felt it was going to be cold, colder than ever before. I began to wonder what would happen to me. And to Father. How would we live from now on? Who would cook for us, wash our clothes? How could life have taken such a strange turn? I went to the kitchen, collected everything I could find to eat, carried it to my room and locked myself in. I decided to stay in the room until the liquid in the jar cleared and I could discuss all these questions with Abortus. There were only two of us now; I couldn't talk to anyone else.

25

Father returned an hour later. I heard the familiar scrabbling sound of the car tires on the gravel in the driveway. I heard him switch off the engine, open the door, slam it shut, walk slowly to the door, unlock it and open it. I heard him go into the kitchen, open the fridge, take out a bottle of wine, uncork it and pour himself a glass. Then I heard him pace restlessly around the living room for what must have over half an hour. Finally I heard the creaking of stairs as he walked up to his library. Soon the sound of music could be heard through the ceiling. For quite some time he had been listening to only one piece, often repeating it endlessly: the third movement of Beethoven's *Ninth Symphony*. The library was above my room, I could hear the boards creaking as he walked up and down. Then the music stopped, and so did the creaking. I thought I heard quiet sobbing. I wasn't used to hearing Father cry, so I was quite relieved when the music resumed.

Then I heard the doorbell. I thought that Father probably couldn't hear it, the music was rather loud. But I did not want to leave my room. The ringing was repeated, this time more insistent. The music above me stopped, Father came creaking down the stairs, I heard him open the door. Judging by the voice that greeted him it was Grandpa Dominic. Almost instinctively I flew to the door, but my hand paused on the key just before turning it. What would I say to him, what would I say to Father? Would I say anything at all? And if Grandpa Dominic wanted to see me, he would ask for me; he must have come to see Father, although I could not imagine why.

I heard them talking in the living room. Father had closed the door behind them, so I could hear only muffled voices; I couldn't make out what they were saying. All I could determine was that it was Grandpa Dominic who did most of the talking. Judging by the tone of his voice he was exhorting Father to do something. A few minutes later I heard them come out of the living room and go outside. Looking out of the window, I saw them walking among the trees toward the small shed at the bottom of the orchard.

I was surprised to see Grandpa Dominic wearing his uniform, cap and all. I was equally surprised to see Father still wearing his white coat, which he must have forgotten to take off as he left the surgery. They walked very slowly and in step, Grandpa Dominic tall and straight, with the dignity of a captain in charge of a sinking boat, and Father stooped, as if carrying a great burden. His gait was a little unsteady, I couldn't tell whether from he wine or anything else.

They stopped in front of the shed. Father produced a key, removed the padlock, opened the door, disappeared inside and almost immediately came out again with two notebooks, which he handed to Grandpa Dominic. He relocked the shed, and slowly they began to walk back to the house. They stared at the ground in front of their feet. Grandpa Dominic folded the two notebooks and pushed them into his side pocket, with half of them sticking out. They looked very much like my dream diaries. They had similar covers, one yellow, and one red. As they passed the window, I saw that neither of them looked very happy.

When they returned into the living room, Father left the door open. I began to hope that I would at last hear what they were saying. But they said nothing for almost five minutes. Then Father said that he would make a telephone call. He walked to the rear of the living room and dialled a number. Again I could not hear the words clearly enough, all I could gather was that he was explaining something and giving our home address, which he repeated twice. He replaced the receiver; then there was silence. After a while they began to speak once again. This time I did not want to miss anything, so I quietly unlocked the door of my room, pushed it open just enough to squeeze out into the hall, and crept as far as the half-open door of the living room, stopping behind it.

"Let me read you, while we wait, a little passage from a book by Robert A. Johnson," I heard Father say.

There was a pause, and because Grandpa Dominic did not object, Father began to read.

"We have reached a point at which we try to get by without acknowledging the inner life at all. We act as though there were no unconscious, no realm of the soul, as though we could live full lives by fixating ourselves completely on the external, material world, making more money, getting more power, starting a love affair. But we discover to our surprise that the inner world is a reality that we ultimately have to face."

"Yes," said Grandpa Dominic, "interesting."

"But I always knew that," Father said. "So how is it possible that, step by unnoticed step, this knowledge seeped out of me, and was replaced by a belief that I could serve my desires and the needs of other people at the same time?"

"Hard to say," said Grandpa Dominic dryly.

"It wasn't my son who was dreaming. I was the one who lost his grip on reality, dreaming that my actions were one thing, and I as a person another."

"What can I say," responded Grandpa Dominic.

"My dreams are over now," Father said after a pause. "They ended when I realized what I had done. I used to grow bonsai plants in the basement. Forcing them into unusual, but visually stunning shapes. I did not realize that my soul was growing into an equally twisted shape, only ugly."

"Nothing much to be done now," Grandpa Dominic said.

"No," Father agreed. "Except one thing."

As Father got to his feet I darted back into my room and turned the key in the lock. I heard Father creak up the stairs again. I heard him moving from room to room, first to the library, then to the bedroom, then to the bathroom and back to the bedroom, opening and closing wardrobes and chests of drawers, as if looking for something, collecting things or changing clothes. Then I heard him coming down again, carrying something heavy.

Then everything happened very quickly, much too quickly for me to react. First there was the scrabbling sound of car tyres on the gravel, then a speeding car came to a screeching halt in front of the house, two doors were opened and slammed shut again.

Someone rang the bell. Father opened the door and I heard a rapid exchange of words. Then the front door was closed and I heard steps moving away.

I expected to hear the car doors again, but instead I heard the squealing of the lid of the metal rubbish container. As if someone had opened it and was taking something out. Then the lid fell back in its place with the familiar twang. Only then did I hear three car doors being slammed one after another. Almost at the same moment the car reversed, made a turn and sped off down the driveway so fast that I heard gravel flying from under the spinning tires.

I pressed my face to the window. I was too late; the car had already turned onto the road and vanished behind the hedge.

26

There was a knock. I bolted to the door to unlock it. With my hand on the key, I paused to take a deep breath. I did not want Grandpa Dominic to see me distraught. When I finally opened the door I found his face looking down at me with the same expression of kindness as always, although there was sadness in his eyes I had not seen before. And a shadow of unusual anger and exasperation, which was not directed at me.

"Adam," he said. "I'm expecting an important delivery. A truck will have to be unloaded. Will you come and help me?"

I nodded, overjoyed at the prospect. I immediately sat down on the bed and started to put on my shoes. Grandpa Dominic stood in the doorway, watching me.

"Have you got a travelling bag?" he asked. When I nodded, he continued, "Put some things in it, a change of clothes, extra socks, whatever you need for school. Unloading will take a while, no point in you going back and forth, far easier if you stay with me."

And then, as an afterthought, "You can sleep in Eve's room."

For the first time in ages my heart was flooded with a wave of pure joy. To spend a few days with Grandpa Dominic in his house – it sounded too good to be true! The travelling bag was ready in less than five minutes.

I pointed to the glass jar on the cabinet. "I'd like to take Abortus with me, if I may. For the last fifteen years he has lived in formaldehyde. He is going through a patch of bad weather right now, but this will clear up. I can't leave him alone."

"In that case," Grandpa Dominic said, "let him come with us."

And so we set off. Grandpa Dominic carried my travelling bag, and I carried Abortus, pressing the glass jar to my stomach with both hands, treading carefully lest I stumbled and fell on top of the jar, breaking it. Grandpa Dominic adjusted his steps to mine, and so we slowly proceeded along narrow field paths toward his house. We met very few people, but those we did were visibly startled, and even stared after us. A grey-bearded sea captain in an elegant uniform with golden insignia, wearing a large cap with a silver-plated shield, two hundred miles from the nearest sea, could not have been an ordinary sight. If the liquid in the jar hadn't turned cloudy, and they could have seen Abortus as well, most would have thought that we had stepped out of a fairy-tale.

"What about Father?" I asked.

Grandpa Dominic said nothing for a long time. He produced an uncertain cough, as if looking for words. When he finally spoke he did not look at me. "Father will be away for some time. It's true he left without saying good-bye, but he was in a great hurry. He was running late for the special seminar he had been asked to attend. Some medical thing, I couldn't really tell you exactly."

"How long will he be away?" I asked. "A few weeks? Months?"

"Oh," Grandpa Dominic shrugged, "more likely years, I'd say."

"Mother is away, too," I said. "She's gone to look after Aunt Yolanda, who is very ill. Can I stay with you until they both return?"

"Of course, Adam," he ruffled my hair. "You can stay with me until I leave for my final voyage."

"When will that be?"

He gave a quiet laugh. "Not so soon, I hope."

As we approached the house we could see a large petrol tanker standing on the road right in front of it.

"We're in time," said Grandpa Dominic.

But the truck driver disagreed, saying that he had been waiting for almost an hour, and was just about to turn around and take "the whole bloody thing" back.

"That would be a great pity," said Grandpa Dominic.

"Adam," he turned to me, "take your things to Eve's room, which will be yours from now on. In the meantime this gentleman and I will try to work out the best way to accomplish what promises to be a complicated manoeuvre."

He passed me the bag. "Will you manage?"

Although it wasn't easy, I managed to get the jar and the bag as far as the big room with the African gods, where I placed Abortus on the oak table. I noticed that the three missing gods were back in their places. Then I carried my bag to the first floor and opened the door to Eve's room.

The teddy bear was sitting in the middle of the bed and staring at me with its plastic eyes as if surprised to see me. I went down on my knees and dug my nose into the bed cover, hoping to trace any remaining smells of Eve, of her skin, of her hair. But all I could smell was dust which had accumulated in the blanket.

Suddenly I was overcome by complete exhaustion. I could almost feel the energy draining out of me. I fell asleep where I was, kneeling on the floor, resting my head on my arms, which I had crossed on the bed. It wasn't a deep sleep, it was more a strange hovering on the border between sleep and wakefulness, and all the time I remained half aware of something going on behind the house. I heard the engine of the truck which kept moving backwards and forwards as if manoeuvring into place, then I heard unfamiliar whirring, splashing and gurgling, then some winding and metal banging, and finally two male voices, shouting and arguing, until finally the engine ran freely for some minutes before revving up again and moving away, followed by silence.

I was woken by Grandpa Dominic, who was standing above me, still wearing his uniform.

"Adam," he said, "why don't you lie on the bed? Have a proper rest. I wanted to show you something, but it can wait."

"No," I rubbed my eyes and got to my feet, "I'm not really sleepy, it's too early. Show me, please."

"All right, come with me."

I followed him downstairs and through the rear door into the courtyard and through the orchard to the small pond among the trees. The truck's wheels had left deep tracks in the soft ground. The water in the pond was of unusual colour, probably because of the fading daylight.

"Something strange has happened," said Grandpa Dominic. "The water has changed its taste. Dip you finger in it and taste it."

I did so, and licked the finger. "This water is salty," I said.

"That's what I thought myself," he said. "We've got sea water in our pond. How could that have happened?"

"It was brought by the tanker," I suggested.

He winked at me; he was again the old sea captain in whose presence I had always felt so secure.

"Right," he said. "That's why it took me such a long time to get back from the seaside. It's only water, but it took days to organise transport. But now we have our own private sea. Inland waters, puddles and ponds get filthy and sour, they begin to stink, and all kinds of vermin appear in them. Only the sea is clean, Adam. Now even the African gods no longer want to desert me. They can feel the purity of this water. Now they will guard the house and both of us and our little sea with all their heart."

As we walked back to the house he said, "I know what people are going to say. The old man has gone senile and childish. But what do they know? Right, Adam? What do they know about the pleasures of being different? We mustn't pay any attention to what they say. They'll be saying things about you and your Father, too. We will ignore all of that, won't we, Adam?"

I nodded. Grandpa Dominic put his hand round my shoulder and asked, "Have I ever told you the legend about the Morsi?"

I shook my head.

"How could I have forgotten?" he slapped his forehead. "I heard the legend in Polynesia, where one of my ships ran aground on a desert island. The Polynesians have many legends, but this one appealed to me most. The Morsi are sea creatures which..."

He suddenly stopped, as if afraid that he was about to divulge a secret for which the African gods might punish him.

"Actually," he said as we reached the door, "it's too dangerous to talk about the Morsi too much. It's nicer and safer to dream about them. I'm sure you'll meet them in your dreams as soon as you fall asleep."

"Are you sure, Grandpa Dominic?"

"Absolutely. And the first dream in a new home is very important, because it contains the seeds of your future. So you must try to remember it."

We stopped in front of the oak table in the big room. The glass jar containing Abortus was standing on it under the watchful eyes of the gods. In semi-darkness their eyes no longer seemed as harsh as before, they had softened and become almost friendly. And if I had ever doubted their unusual powers I had no reason to do so any more: the liquid inside the jar had miraculously cleared, and Abortus was once again able to look at the world around him!

"My little brother," I introduced him to Grandpa Dominic.

He bent down to take a closer look. I wasn't quite sure, but it seemed to me that he was a little startled.

"Can't see much resemblance," he said. "But very often those who have most in common resemble each other least."

"Can he stay here?" I asked. "On this table? With the gods?"

"Well," Grandpa Dominic straightened up and coughed slightly, "I can see no reason why not. We're unlikely to have many visitors, so there is little chance that anyone would suffer a heart attack. Actually he is quite likeable."

He asked me if I wanted to eat or drink anything before going to bed, but I was in a hurry to fall asleep and start dreaming about the Morsi. I asked him if they resembled sharks in any way.

"Not at all," said Grandpa Dominic and sank into the armchair next to the oak table. "The Morsi are creatures of unconditional goodness. They keep cleansing the oceans. That is why the sea never gets dirty. Sometimes, if you feel very unhappy, one of them may allow you to touch him. After that you never feel lonely any more."

His hand felt around for the cigar box; when I saw that he couldn't reach it, I pushed it toward him. As he opened it and took out a cigar I saw that his hand was trembling.

"And now, dear Adam, the old captain is getting tired. No longer able to deal with dangerous storms as he used to in his younger days. And this storm has been one of the worst."

He lit the cigar and pushed the extinguished match in the breast pocket of his jacket. He drew on the cigar, blew the smoke toward the ceiling and gave a sigh of contentment.

"Will your little brother mind if I have a smoke every now and then?" he suddenly remembered.

I said that he most certainly wouldn't. On the contrary, for the first time in fifteen years he would feel really secure and happy.

"What about you?" asked Grandpa Dominic, as if in passing. But I felt that he was quite interested in hearing my answer.

"Me too," I assured him.

"All right, then," he said, leaning back and resting his head on the back of the chair. "Go now and dream about the Morsi."

He closed his eyes and looked as if he was about to fall asleep. I carefully pulled the cigar from his hand and put it out by pushing the burning end against the table leg. Grandpa Dominic's hand came to rest on his knee. He was breathing slowly and peacefully.

I said good night to Abortus and went up to my room. I put Eve's teddy bear on the chest of drawers. I took off my shoes, undressed, fished pyjamas from my bag, put them on and climbed into bed. I remembered Eve. I felt warm and comfortable. I decided to ask Grandpa Dominic where she was being treated, when he thought they would release her, when she would visit him.

I tried to imagine her lying next to me, with both of us sinking into sleep hand in hand. And suddenly there we were, outside in the orchard, next to the pond with sea water, for the first time in a dream without Father. The pond widened into a sea which seemed to be endless, with frothy waves travelling away from the land into space.

And then I suddenly saw them. There were four of them, and they came running out of the sea with synchronised movements, as if performing a carefully choreographed ballet, all of the same size, resembling sheep dogs with very long hair, but with heads which reminded me of smiling dolphins. Although they had come from the sea they were not wet, and their bodies, although alive, looked transparent, as if made of glass. One was glassy blue, another glassy white, the third glassy red, the fourth silvery. As soon as they reached the land they stopped moving in unison and began to run around freely, jumping up and down, rolling about in the grass, sitting and staring, then rushing back to the water, splashing about in the shallows, and racing back out again.

The glassy white one sat down in front of us, watching us with the twinkling eyes of a dolphin. Grandpa Dominic came out of the house and brought a loaf of bread. He divided it into three pieces and gave one to Eve and one to me. We squatted, and the Morsi gathered in front of us, eating bread from our hands. Their snouts felt soft and caressing, but cold. When they finished the bread they leapt to their feet to run back into the sea.

But the glassy white one remained sitting in front of us. He was in no hurry to leave. The other three paused to wait for him. I slowly approached, and he allowed me to stroke his head. Then Eve did the same. Now we will never feel lonely again, I remembered Grandpa Dominic's words. Then the Morsi wagged their tails as if to say good-bye, and in the same way they had come, with synchronised movements, raced back into the sea.

Sifting through these diary notes on board a merchant ship sailing toward Polynesia, and trying to give them a coherent shape which would finally allow me to put them aside for good, I keep looking at the rolling breakers of the ocean, still waiting after all these years for the head of a Morsi to appear on the surface. I have been doing that ever since I became the skipper of a medium-sized vessel transporting spices in one direction, and electronic devices in the other. So far I have not seen one, but I keep hoping that one day, when I least expect it, the glassy white one, the one I touched, will push its dolphin head out of the water and confirm my belief that there is little to distinguish dreams from reality, and that in many cases they can be one and the same.

I keep hoping that everything these notes contain is true in a wider sense than simply as a record of a childhood impossible to forget. The waters of the ocean are clean and sparkling, and I have not seen land for weeks. The crew find me a little strange; unlike them, I do not look forward to reaching port. I am never lonely; the photo of Captain Dominic which hangs on the wall of my cabin is enough to remind me that one's own company is as good as any, and a lot better than the company of those who have not left the shallows of the known.

THE AUTHOR

Evald Flisar (1945, Slovenia)

Novelist, playwright, essayist, editor, globe-trotter (having travelled in more than 90 countries), Flisar worked as an underground train driver in Sydney, an editor of (among other publications) an encyclopaedia of science and invention in London, an author of short stories and radio plays for the BBC, president of the Slovene Writers' Association (1995– 2002). Since 1998 he has been the chief editor of the oldest Slovenian literary journal Sodobnost (Contemporary Review). He is the author of 12 novels (eight of them short-listed for the 'Kresnik' prize, the Slovenian "Booker"), two collections of short stories, three travelogues, two books for children, and fifteen stage plays (seven nominated for Best Play of the Year Award, three winners). He is also the recipient of the Prešeren Foundation Prize, the highest state award for prose and drama and the prestigious Župančič Award for lifetime achievement. His various works translated into 34 languages, among them Bengali, Malay, Nepalese, Indonesian, Turkish, Greek, Japanese, Chinese, Arabic, Czech, Albanian, Lithuanian, Icelandic, Romanian, Amharic, Russian, English, German, Italian and Spanish. His stage plays are regularly performed all over the world, most recently in Austria, Egypt, India, Indonesia, Japan, Taiwan, Serbia, Bosnia, Bulgaria and Belarus. Throughout his career he has attended more than 50 literary readings and festivals on all continents. After a long period of life abroad (three years in Australia, 17 years in London), Flisar has been resident in Ljubljana, Slovenia, since 1990. In 2014, his novel 'On the Gold Coast' (published in English by Sampark, Kolkata, India) has been nominated for the most prestigious European literary prize, the Dublin IMPAC International Literary Award.